Woof. Meow. You're dead.

She took a step or two backwards, and would have turned and run unthinkingly back along the path into the wood, but a soft bark made her turn and swing the light. Another cat-dog was behind her.

Sheer terror gave her the courage to run forward on the path home, swinging the torch at the cat-dog that blocked her way. The animal dodged the blow neatly and then, with a dancing step, darted in and drove its teeth into her forearm. . . .

Other Thrillers
you will enjoy:

Driver's Dead
by Peter Lerangis

The Stranger
by Caroline B. Cooney

Be Mine
by Jane McFann

Thirteen
edited by T. Pines

THE CAT-DOGS

Edited by A. Finnis

SCHOLASTIC INC.
New York Toronto London Auckland Sydney

ISBN 0-590-22292-9

First published in 1994 by Scholastic Publications Limited. This anthology copyright © 1994 by Scholastic Publications Limited. All rights reserved. Published by Scholastic Inc., 555 Broadway, New York, NY 10012, by arrangement with Scholastic Publications Limited.

12 11 10 9 8 7 6 5 4 3 2   5 6 7 8 9/9 0/0

Printed in U.S.A.

First Scholastic printing, August 1995

Acknowledgments

Contents

Contents

THE CAT-DOGS

Susan Price

THE CAT-DOGS HAD EATEN EVERYTHING EX-
cept a beak, a pair of web-footed legs, and
some white feathers. Liz was thankful that she
was the first to discover the duck's remains.

She was in the kitchen-garden, a big walled
area of neat vegetable plots and gravelled
paths. She kicked the feathers about so they
wouldn't be noticed, and then gathered up the
beak and legs. On the other side of the high
brick wall at the far end of the garden was a
motorway. She tossed the remains over the
wall. They would land on the motorway's
verge and never be noticed. Resisting the
temptation to wipe her hands on her clothes,
she ran back to the kitchen to wash.

She knew it had been the cat-dogs who had
eaten the duck. The Bowyers' Alsatian, Tom,
was too well trained to chase poultry, and the
farm cats had long ago learned that they were

no match for the flock of geese, ducks, chickens and turkeys that strutted about the farmyard. Liz felt guilty about the cat-dogs — she had been the one who had brought them to the farm. Her father had never blamed her, but every time the cat-dogs killed a duck or a chicken, when they chased and bit the sheep and killed a lamb, or when they got ambitious and harried the cows, she felt that it was her fault.

She'd found them on her way home from school the year before. Once she parted from her friends on the main road, her walk home was a solitary one along a road which made its way between factories before abruptly turning into something like a country lane. On one side were the woods, on the other a landscaped park which swept down to the motorway and the town beyond. The great house of an earl had once stood here, in its park. Now the council owned what was left of the estate and ran it as a nature reserve. The earl's home-farm had become a tourist attraction and the woods were a playground for local children and dogs. But though they worked the farm as it had been worked in Victorian times, though they were bringing back old woodland crafts, the roar of the traffic on the motorway never stopped, night or day.

Liz had climbed a stile into the woods, but had then turned aside from the main bridle-path, which would have taken her in a direct fashion through a mile of woodland, past the abbey-ruins and the holy well, to the farm. It was a path much used by horse-riders and walkers, and it bored her. Instead she had taken a narrower, winding path that wandered through more overgrown parts of the wood and, at one point, brought her to the edge of the lake. There, on a little sandy beach under a dark green holly bush, she'd found the sodden, squeaking sack, and had clambered down the bank to rescue it.

She'd thought the little animals inside were kittens. They'd looked more like kittens then — gingerish, tabby and snub-nosed. There'd been something odd about them, but she hadn't thought much about it. She'd been too angry with whoever had stuffed them in the sack and thrown them in the water to drown. She'd scrambled back up the bank with the sack and carried them home with great

care. In the stable at home she knew there
was a mother cat with kittens who would look
after them.

She'd found her mother in the farmyard, and
had put the sack down on the cobbles and taken
out the little animals. Word went round. The
women from the tea shop came out in relays
to look. Her father had appeared, bringing one
of the gardeners with him, and the girl from
the gift shop had come running down to see.
There hadn't been many visitors to the farm
at the time — a family of Japanese tourists and
a couple of local mothers with small children —
but they had all gathered round and stared.
Everyone had agreed that the animals must
be cats of some kind.

"Perhaps they're wild cats?" someone had
suggested.

"Grey," her father had said, meaning that
wild cats were grey not ginger. "Kinder to
have let 'em drown," he said to Liz.

"The mother cat in the stable will look after
them," Liz said.

He shook his head. "Got her own kittens."

But Liz had gone ahead, and put the little
ginger kittens in with the mother cat's black
and white ones. The next morning, all the

black and white kittens had been dead, their tiny bodies covered with innumerable bites, their fur matted with dried blood. The question of how they'd died had been much discussed. Liz, for one, was convinced rats had killed them. Mr. Bowyer didn't argue, but it was plain he didn't agree. Mrs. Bowyer, frankly, wasn't very interested. She had enough to do, she said, looking after the business of the farm, and her own family, without worrying about the family of a stable-cat. She'd had to phone Iceland again about those blasted sheep.

Liz had laughed and said, "Dad's set on those sheep!"

"Ancient breeds," said her mother, and quoted her husband: " 'When plagues and murrains sweep the world and wipe out our present stock, we're going to need them.' "

Liz grinned. Her mother was just as enthusiastic as her father about turning the show-farm into a haven for ancient breeds, and just as proud of their black Tamworth pigs, their Gloucester Old Spots, their Clydesdale Shire horses, Shropshire sheep, Aylesbury ducks and Indian game fowl. She only complained because she was feeling a bit overworked. "How's it going?"

"Oh — red tape and paperwork. Permission to bring them out of Iceland. Permission to bring them into Britain. Certificates of health, freight charges — I wish people wouldn't put these ideas into your dad's head."

"It was probably you!" Liz said, and her mother smiled and nodded.

While Mrs. Bowyer struggled with the regulations, phoned Iceland every week, and tried to convince the council that Icelandic sheep were necessary to the farm's success, the ginger kittens suckled at the mother cat, and were weaned, and grew bigger.

Nobody was quite sure what they were growing into. "They're never cats!" said Betty from the tea shop. "Never in a month of Sundays are they cats."

Mr. Bowyer spent hours watching them, in the evenings, when the farm had closed and the staff and the visitors had gone home. A low wall separated what had once been the farmhouse — and was now the tea shop and the Bowyers' flat — from the rest of the yard, and he would sit on the wall with his mug of tea and a sandwich, watching the strange little creatures play with the mother cat and with Tom.

"Their teeth aren't cat's teeth," he said. "More like a dog's."

Liz nodded. "Their noses are more like dogs'. More pointed."

Mrs. Bowyer was sitting with them, sipping at a hot mug of tea. "Their coats are like ginger tabbies, though."

They watched the five "kittens" stalking Tom. One crept up on him from behind, while two came at him from the front, and two more ran in from the side. Tom put down his nose and sniffed at them, wagging his tail. He yelped as one chewed on his hind leg.

"They're rangier then cats," Mr. Bowyer said.

Liz said, "But they're like Siamese cats. Y'know, the black ears and black legs, and black tips to their tails."

"Siamese don't have bushy tails like that."

"No, but dogs don't have green eyes." All the "kittens" had bright green or yellow eyes.

"And retractable claws," her father said. "No animal except a cat has retractable claws." Anyone who had tried playing with the "kittens" could testify to the cat-like fineness and sharpness of their claws.

"And the noises they make," Mrs. Bowyer

said. "All those mews and squeaks. Just like cats."

Mr. Bowyer shook his head. "But they bark as well, not like dogs. Like foxes. And they hunt like — like wolves! Look!" The kittens were herding a group of geese around the yard. The geese, big birds which would stand their ground and drive off people, let alone cats and dogs, were flustered by the sudden darts made at them from several different directions. While the birds flapped and honked and scurried in all directions, the cat-dogs kept low, running forward with their bellies almost on the cobbles. Watching them, Liz suddenly shuddered: there was something so intent, so sinister about those rapid, scuttling movements.

Two geese and a duck separated from the main flock, and all five cat-dogs turned their attention to this little group. Two moved in from one side and a third moved from the other side, while the remaining two hung back. As neatly as sheep-dogs following a shepherd's orders, they separated the duck from the geese — and the two cat-dogs who had hung back moved smoothly in to pen the duck in a corner.

"Oh no, you don't!" Mr. Bowyer rose from the wall and strode across the yard, stamping his feet on the cobbles and clapping his hands. Startled, the cat-dogs re-grouped and shied away from him. He drove them through the archway that led from the walled farmyard to the big kitchen-gardens and came back after a few minutes, having driven them out into the woods.

"Can't have them thinking they can hunt the poultry," he said, coming back to his mug of tea.

"They're beautiful though," Liz said.

"Freaks — some kind of freaks."

"Have you seen the double-takes the visitors do when they see 'em?" her mother asked. "Oh, that reminds me! Can we put an Icelandic vet up for a day or two, do you think?"

"If he brings the sheep, I'll house him for a month," Mr. Bowyer said, and they went indoors to talk over possible dates. Liz stayed on the wall and watched the kittens creep back into the yard. Cats, but not quite cats. Like dogs, but not dogs. Cat-dogs. Once she started using it, the name was taken up by everyone else on the farm, and stuck.

It was soon a name spoken with nothing but dislike, because, as the cat-dogs grew older still, they left the farmyard and took to the woods and fields. They were seen less often, but they left signs — like the remains of the duck Liz had found. More than once the little pale-brown Jersey cows had been found sweating and unsettled, trembling with exhaustion after being harried all night. And a little newborn lamb, dead and ripped open and partly eaten, is something that enrages most people — more especially the farmer who had the trouble of caring for it.

"If this was a commercial farm . . ." Mr. Bowyer said. He wanted to kill the cat-dogs, put out poisoned bait, trap them. But that wasn't possible on a show farm, run for tourists in the middle of a nature reserve where people came to walk their dogs and brought their children to play. Even taking out a shotgun late at night and trying to shoot the cat-dogs was risky — the shot might wing a courting couple. So the poultry and the sheep had to be penned every night. "As if I haven't enough to do!" Mr. Bowyer said.

"You've got your packing as well," his wife

said. "You've got to go down to Heathrow, remember."

Mrs. Bowyer's persistence and countless phone calls had paid off at last. Sven Ivarssen was flying into Heathrow with three sheep, and would be delayed there while the animals were inspected for disease. It seemed only hospitable for Mr. Bowyer to drive down to meet him, staying overnight.

Liz thought it all very exciting. An evening meal spent alone with her mother was a novelty. Somehow, despite the flats and office-blocks in the middle-distance, despite the motorway at the bottom of the kitchen-garden, the farm seemed very isolated without her father's presence. Anyone could come wandering through these woods, she thought. It made her nervous to think of herself and her mother all alone in the woods, but it gave her a thrill too.

And then, tomorrow, her father would be coming back, not only with three new animals, of a breed unchanged for a thousand years, but with a real live Icelander too. "A Viking and his viking sheep," she said to her mother. "He vill be six feet five mit lonk blont hair unt a hat mit horns!"

"What, the sheep?" her mother said, and shook her head. She had spoken to Sven Ivarssen on the phone. "You might be disappointed."

The day turned out to be a lot more exciting than Liz liked.

She usually woke early, and took a walk around the farm before the staff and visitors arrived. The early morning and the evening were the only times she could pretend that the farm was really theirs.

At night, with all the gates locked, the big farmyard with the tall buildings on all four sides became a fortress. Keys in hand, Liz walked along to the archway and unlocked the big door. That brought her out into the flower-garden where the visitors sat over their "farm-house teas." A path led through the flower borders to the gate of the much bigger kitchen-gardens. It was here, in the gardens, that Tom spent his nights, on guard. A small gate in the garden wall was usually left open, so that he could come and go to investigate any noise. Liz called for him as she walked into the garden.

He didn't come to her call, but that didn't

worry her. He might be anywhere, in the fields or woods. She walked over to the gate, meaning to take a stroll around the farm buildings, and perhaps go a little way into the wood before returning to breakfast.

Tom was lying on his back just outside the gate. She knew as soon as she saw him that he was dead: there was that peculiar, broomstick stiffness about his splayed legs. One of the dog's hind legs looked strange and, after staring for a long time, she realized that the flesh had been dragged away from the bone. She turned and ran back through the garden, through the archway, into the yard and back into the flat, shouting for her mother.

While Liz remained at a distance, Mrs. Bowyer crouched beside Tom and turned the carcase over, examining it closely. She made Liz feel cowardly.

"Still got the keys?" her mother asked. "Open the shed, will you?" There was a little wooden shed against the wall, just behind the garden gate. Liz opened it, and turned to see her mother carrying Tom's body towards her. She turned away hastily, afraid of what she might see.

Her mother put the dog's body in the shed,

took the keys from Liz and locked the door. "Can't leave him for the tourists to fall over, can we?" She spoke through her teeth. From the shed she took a spade, and turned over the blood-stained soil where Tom had lain. Everything must be nice for the tourists.

"What do you think killed him?" Liz asked, her voice strained and shaky.

Her mother glanced at her, as if wondering if she should tell her the truth. Then she said, "The cat-dogs. What else around here would take on an Alsatian? He was — no. Let's not talk about it until your dad comes back. Let's go and have a good hot cup of tea."

Liz drank a mug of tea but didn't feel much like breakfast. Her mother said that she needn't go to school if she didn't want to, but she already felt like a ninny for being afraid to look at Tom. She packed her satchel and set off, as usual, through the woods, but she didn't even get halfway. She felt shaky and upset, and couldn't bear the thought of trying to get through a noisy school day — and she couldn't stop thinking about the cat-dogs. These were gentle English woods, with broad paths, but they were also very lonely at that time in the morning. No walkers, no riders. The cat-dogs were about, though. They ran in the woods now. And if they could hunt down and kill a big, strong Alsatian, a dog who had been far stronger than Liz . . .

She turned and hurried home to the farm, thankful to get there without hearing the cat-dogs running behind her, without hearing their barks. She spent the day half-heartedly helping in the shop, trying not to think of Tom or the cat-dogs, and envying the visitors who didn't know about them. "Your dad'll be back soon," her mother said.

He arrived at about three that afternoon and for an hour Liz was happy and excited. A van drove up outside the farm and her father jumped out, shouting for keys. The big gates of the farmyard were unlocked, and the van was driven inside and pulled up beside the open-sided animal sheds that lined one side of the yard. A crowd of interested onlookers had gathered, Mrs. Bowyer and Liz among them.

Her father let down the back of the van. "Icelandic sheep!" he cried. The sheep, when they were coaxed out, were small, with shaggy grey-brown wool. The ram had big curly horns.

Mr. Bowyer asked people to stand well back

as he and a stranger guided the sheep gently into one of the sheds and penned them in with hurdles. They were left there, with food and water, to settle in, while Mr. Bowyer led the stranger forward. "Sven — let me introduce you to the best wife and daughter a man ever had."

Far from being six foot five and blond, Sven was about five foot eight, and his mousey-brown hair was balding at the front. He seemed much younger than Mr. Bowyer, perhaps in his late twenties, and he had a nice, rather shy smile. "Very pleased to meet you," he said, shaking hands with Mrs. Bowyer and Liz. "Very kind of you to put me up." His English had a slight American accent.

When were they going to get a chance to tell her father about Tom? Liz was wondering, because he was insisting on showing Sven round the farm at once, and was taking him by the arm to lead him over to the sty of Tamworth pigs.

"Poor Sven!" Mrs. Bowyer said. "I'm sure he'd like a cup of tea first, and a look at the *very* Old English sofa-bed he's going to have to sleep on?" Mr. Bowyer reluctantly allowed

Sven to be taken from him and led into the flat.

While their guest was "washing his hands," Liz and her mother told Mr. Bowyer what had happened. When Sven came out 'of the bathroom, Mr. Bowyer was swearing and thumping the window-frames. Sven looked as if he would turn and lock himself in the bathroom again.

"Oh, it's all right!" Mrs. Bowyer called out. "It's just something that came up while Bob was away. Our dog's been killed."

Sven came forward. "Your dog! I'm sorry to hear that!" He looked at Liz, and she tried to be brave and smile. "Was he knocked by a car?"

"Cat-dogs!" Mr. Bowyer said, and Sven looked bewildered, especially when he saw the faces of Liz and Mrs. Bowyer.

"You're a vet," Mr. Bowyer said suddenly. "Where did you say you'd put Tom, love? In the shed? Come and have a look, Sven — give us your opinion, as a vet."

Sven still looked bewildered, but followed Mr. Bowyer out into the yard. Mrs. Bowyer went with them, and Liz found herself trailing along behind. She didn't want to see Tom, dead, and with bites all over him, but she didn't want to be left out either.

Mrs. Bowyer opened the shed and stood aside. She wasn't keen to see Tom again either. Mr. Bowyer and Sven went into the shed and squatted on their heels as Sven examined the dog's body. Liz stood at a little distance, looking at their bowed backs. She heard Sven say, "Bites."

The two men got to their feet and came out of the shed. Sven pushed the door of the shed closed and looked at the ground.

"So . . . what do you think?" Mr. Bowyer asked.

"The dog was attacked by — animals," Sven said. "By other dogs I would make the guess."

Mr. and Mrs. Bowyer looked at each other. "Cat-dogs," Mr. Bowyer said.

Sven looked from one to another of them. "They don't look quite like dogs or like cats," Mrs. Bowyer explained.

"Teeth like dogs," Mr. Bowyer said, "but claws like cats."

Liz saw Sven raise his head, and his expression quickened. "And red," he said. "Red, like a fox."

"Yes," Mrs. Bowyer said. "But tabby — you know, striped — like a cat."

It was odd, but Sven was looking increasingly uneasy. The tip of his tongue came out between his lips, and he wouldn't look at them. "Skoffins!" he breathed.

Mr. and Mrs. Bowyer both said, "What?" and Liz took a step nearer.

"Skoffins," Sven repeated. "Cat-dogs you call them in England?"

The Bowyers all looked at each other. "That's just what *we* call 'em," Mr. Bowyer said. "We don't know what you're talking about."

Sven sighed. "Let's go to the house — and I will tell you."

Once back in the house, Mrs. Bowyer made coffee, and they sat around the kitchen table and looked expectantly at Sven. He seemed embarrassed. "I think you will laugh at me. Even in Iceland, people laugh sometimes . . . People in Reykjavik, not farmers . . ."

"We like a laugh," Mrs. Bowyer said. "Tell us."

"Your dog didn't laugh!" Sven said. "You have raised a pack of skoffins, and this is a dangerous thing."

"What is a skoffin?" Liz said.

Sven began his explanation, directing his words at Liz. "In Iceland," he said, "there are many lonesome farms . . . and many foxes. In Icelandic, did you know, the word for 'fox' is the same word for 'devil'? And sometimes a fox, a female fox — "

"A vixen," Mrs. Bowyer murmured.

"A vixen, thank you — a vixen will come to a farm and mate with the farm's tom-cat — "

Mr. Bowyer laughed loudly and slapped the table. When they looked at him, he laughed again and said, "Impossible!"

Sven turned to Liz again. "The vixen goes away, and the babies are born wild. They are called skuggabalders, and they are very fierce, very clever. They are rare, but they kill sheep, they kill dogs . . . They are dangerous animals. The farmers get together and shoot them."

"But skoffins?" Liz said.

Sven nodded. "Sometimes a female cat from a farm mates with a . . ." Sven looked at Mrs. Bowyer, who said, "A dog-fox."

Sven waved a hand, to acknowledge her words. "Then the kittens are born on a farm. *They* are called skoffins. But, in Iceland, they never grow up. The farmers kill them as soon as they find them — they say a skoffin is even more clever and even more fierce than a skuggabalder. But you didn't know. You have raised a pack of skoffins."

Mr. Bowyer laughed again. "He's pulling your leg, Liz! Cats and foxes can't mate! They don't belong to the same family."

"I am not pulling anybody's leg," Sven said. Mr. Bowyer, sitting with folded arms, gave him a level stare across the table, waiting for him to admit that he was joking. Sven looked calmly back. He said, "Teeth like a dog; claws like a cat." He looked at Mrs. Bowyer. "Red like a fox, tabby like a cat. Hunts in a pack, like a wolf . . . and killed a big dog."

Mrs. Bowyer said, "Liz has to go through that wood every day to school."

Mr. Bowyer was only silent a moment; then he said, "You ever heard of 'lamping', Sven?" The Icelander shook his head. "You go out at night with a lamp or torch, and you shine it. If you catch a rabbit or a fox — or a skoffin — in the light, they freeze — "

"And then you shoot them," Sven said. "Have you gotten a gun?"

Mr. Bowyer nodded.

As soon as it was fully dark they were ready: Mr. Bowyer with his shotgun and his pockets full of cartridges; Sven with the big electric lamp with carrying handle and cover for the light.

"You coming?" Mr. Bowyer asked Liz.

She nodded.

"I'm not sure I like her going," Mrs. Bowyer said.

"We're not hunting tigers! They're little things, no bigger than foxes."

"A little bigger," Sven said. "As a big domestic cat is bigger and heavier than a fox."

"Still not tigers," Mr. Bowyer said. "Anyway, if she wants to do this sort of job later on . . ."

"I'll be all right, Mum," Liz said. "I'll stick close by Dad and Sven." But she was less happy than she seemed as she followed her father and Sven through the farmyard and out into the wood.

It was easy enough to follow the tracks in the dark, but once they'd crossed the narrow plank bridge over the stream and were into the wood, the trees, meeting over their heads, made walls of dense leaves on either side, shutting out what little light there was. Unable to see the ground at their feet, they stumbled on every hollow or hump, staggered through roots, were caught by briars. Branches lashed out of nowhere across their faces, or caught in their hair and jerked them backwards. It was impossible to move quietly. All around them the wood was silent; but they thrashed, crashed, trampled . . .

Ahead of them, Liz's father swore as his shotgun caught in branches. None of them, she realized, had stopped to think of how difficult it is to move through a wood at night. To make it easier for Sven and herself, she uncovered the lamp and allowed a thin beam of light to fall at their feet. It illuminated tangles of thin twigs and leaves, but made such deep, pit-like shadows that, if anything, it made them even more reluctant to risk another step.

"Cover the light!" her father said. Liz protested that even with the lamp they couldn't see, but her father said, "It's ruining our night-vision."

Liz covered the lamp. Immediately, darkness; such darkness that she stood still, blinded. The darkness and the silence wrapped close around her, like the slight dampness of the air. Ahead of her, seeming very far away, she could hear the crunch and thrash of her father slowly making his way, step by careful step, along the narrow path. It was the other sounds that held her attention: the slight sound of a bird shifting in its roost above her head; the wind trickling through leaves; a scuttering in the bushes beside the path, all fading into the deeper quiet.

From behind her came Sven's whisper: "Liz!" She turned and, unable to see him, un-covered the lamp, hiding its light from her father with her jacket. The beam brought a little patch of woodland out of the darkness: one quivering, emerald leaf, surrounded by leaves and twigs of various greys, and then darkness again. She edged towards the sound of Sven's voice, and bashed her head on a low branch.

Sven was off the path, trapped knee-deep in a clump of brambles and nettles. Dazzling him briefly, she turned the light on the briars so he could untangle himself. "In Iceland," he said, as he pulled at briars and sucked his pricked fingers, "we have no woods." He floundered back to the path and looked up into the dark, breeze-whispering canopies above them, hugging himself. Liz thought she saw him shiver. He glanced at her in the lamp's light, and grinned. "Spooky!" he said.

They edged along the path, following Mr. Bowyer. Liz covered the lamp again so as not to annoy her father. Where was he? She stood still in the darkness, listening for the sound of him moving, but the wood was full of wariness and silence. Her father must be standing still too. Sven, catching her mood, called softly, "Bob!"

They waited, their heads lifted up, but there was no answer. Liz looked back, wondering if they should go back to the farm. But that seemed a stupid waste of time. Her father would come back to them soon. They had the light.

The shotgun blasted in the darkness away to their right; an outcry of birds followed a second later. Both of them started towards the sound. It seemed, to Liz, to come from further away than her father should be. Perhaps it had taken Sven longer than she'd thought to get free of the briars.

As the echoes of the shot died, birds cried in alarm from every part of the wood. There were sounds of scurryings, wings clapping — and then all the sounds of fright began to settle into silence again. Liz flashed the torch-beam about the ground, hoping to see some path leading in the direction of the shot, but the only path seemed to lead away from it. So she left the path and struck out through the undergrowth. It seemed a good idea at the time, and Sven followed her, trampling leaves underfoot.

There seemed nothing in the way except a few low-growing plants, a few bushes — but the ground sloped away suddenly, sending Liz stumbling forward, half-running. Her feet shot from under her and she slithered downhill through leaf-mould, the smell of damp earth rising all around her. In trying to grab at something to stop her fall, she let go of the lamp and left it behind.

When she stopped falling, she was nervy and bruised, and lying in darkness. The last reverberations of the noise she had made were settling. Dozens of tiny scratches burned her face and hands. Getting to her hands and knees, she realized that she hardly knew which way was up, let alone how to get back to the path. The wood — the little toy wood where townies walked dogs — suddenly seemed vast. Not daring to raise her voice much, she called for Sven.

From somewhere — she was too appalled to notice from where — came a sound that went through her like an arrow and had her hugging the ground like every other terrified animal in the wood. It was a twisting, wailing shriek. Her breath came fast.

She wanted to call out for her father and Sven, but feared to make a sound. She lay flat, kept still, and tried not to breathe too loudly. Only when she was still alive three minutes later did her brain begin to work again. She couldn't lie here all night. She shifted her position slightly and caught a gleam of light through the bushes. The lamp! Ignoring the branches and thorns in her way, she crawled towards it. As her hand was reaching out she saw, at the edge of the light, a pair of pricked ears. With a lunge, she grabbed the lamp and turned the light full on the spot. Nothing.

Filling her lungs, she shouted, "Sven!"

"Here!" A shifting and rustling to her left, and Sven came crawling through the dark leaves. She was glad to scramble over and sit next to him. She thought he seemed glad to see her.

"Did you hear that . . . noise?"

She saw him nod in the light of the torch. "A skoffin." He peered about in the dark. "We shouldn't have come into this wood. How do we get out?"

Liz shone the torch about. It showed them so little, and one suddenly illuminated, grey-green tree-trunk looked like another. "I don't know," she said.

Sven got to his feet, put his hands about his mouth and yelled, "Bob!" His voice went clattering through the trees and the darkness. Birds roused, twittered, and fell silent. Liz, still sitting, felt the wood grow tense around her. Everything out there knows exactly where we are, she thought.

Something darker than the darkness moved swiftly through the tangle of bushes near her, and she jumped to her feet and shone the torchlight at that spot. Nothing. But the leaves were still quivering.

"Don't," she said, finding herself rather short of breath. "Don't shout again."

Sven was looking about. "Already they've

separated us. Liz, we must stay together."

The fact that he was scared frightened her. "What about Dad?"

"He has the gun."

Yes, but they hadn't heard anything of him since that last shot. Liz listened. The wood wasn't extensive, however endless it seemed in the darkness, and she thought that she ought to be able to hear her father moving about. He ought to have heard Sven's shout. Why hadn't he answered?

"I think we should try and find Dad." She moved slowly in what she thought was the right direction, though she was no longer sure. Behind her, she could hear Sven following cautiously. With the help of the torch they picked their way around thickets, becoming more and more lost.

Hardly a step behind them, another long shriek clawed through the air — a shriek that might have come from a tortured baby. Liz leapt and spun, trying at the same time to escape the sound and to see what had made it. Sven took her arm in a tight grip. "They are trying to panic us," he said, gasping. Liz could feel her heart hammering in her throat. "They want us to run and scatter," Sven said.

He took a sudden step forward, waving his hands at the undergrowth and shouting. "Yah!"

Behind them, Liz heard a flurry of movement, and turned sharply, shining her torch at the spot. Nothing.

She and Sven came together and stood close. The wood towered around them, and the thick growth about their legs was full of slight sounds and movements. Bold grey tree-trunks emerged suddenly from the darkness at the touch of the torch-beam, and quickly stepped back into the blackness as the light shifted.

"We must get out of this wood," Sven said. "Which way?"

"But my dad — "

"Your dad has his gun."

Liz was about to ask if the cat-dogs were *really* dangerous, when she realized that it was a stupid question, and one that Sven wouldn't want to answer. Instead, she stood quite still and tried to concentrate on the wood and its paths, and the one they had taken from the farm. "I think . . . if we go this way, we'll get to the main path."

It was slow going, even with the lamp. Every step had to be felt for, and their faces guarded from branches. "Why do you think Dad doesn't answer us?" Liz asked.

"He is . . ." Sven said. "He is probably . . ." And then he couldn't think of anything comforting to say. They pushed on, slipping, stumbling, without saying anything more. Liz felt furious with the branches and briars that kept getting in her way. Anger wouldn't help, she knew, but it was hard to hold it down — or was it panic?

"I thought the path . . ." she said. There was still no sign of any path. From their left came a sudden rising chain of quick little yelps — they were answered from their right. Liz almost started to run, but Sven held her arm.

"We mustn't let them drive us," he said.

Liz almost giggled. "Keep calm."

"We must keep calm. And get out of this English wood!"

The ground began to slope again, and their feet slipped in the leaf-mould. They had to cling to trees and wedge their feet against the boles. Liz slung the lamp on her arm, where it lit up her jeans and trainers but left the tangled way ahead in darkness. Behind them the cat-dogs yipped again. She began to sweat with more than exertion. She was trying to think where this slope could be: where, *where* did the wood slope like this? In daylight she had never noticed.

They paused and Liz shone the torch around. It caught the red glare of eyes behind them, and she shouted, and Sven threw twigs and handfuls of leaves. The eyes vanished. The lamp shone ahead of them, lighting up a line of reddish stone.

Liz shone the light on a wall, a corner, the remains of worn steps. "The abbey!" she said, looking up at Sven and grinning. She knew where they were now. They had come blundering out of the wood into the ruins of the abbey. "Listen!" she said, holding up a finger. From the other side of the ruins could be heard the faint trickling of water in St. Braide's holy well. "The main path's by the well — it goes through the wood straight to the farm."

"Through the wood," Sven said doubtfully.

Hearing a sound, Liz turned the light of the torch on the wood behind them. There was a faint yip, and the sound of something moving away. "There's no other way," she said. "But it's a clear path — easy going."

They slithered down the bank on their

haunches, and stepped over the ruined wall into the abbey. "Sanctuary?" Liz said, and then wished that she hadn't. There was no longer any safety in the abbey.

"I hate woods," Sven said.

The rooms of the abbey, outlined by its ruined walls, were filled with big loose chippings of stone, which crunched noisily under their feet and turned their ankles, making the going almost as difficult as in the wood.

"Look!" Liz said. The light from the torch had been streaming ahead of them, across loose stone and black walls. A running shape had suddenly darted across the light, and turned to run back — a jogging, dog-like shape with pricked ears. It looked at them and yipped. It was answered by more calls and barks from the wood. The cat-dogs were on the path ahead of them.

They both moved back, away from the cat-dogs they could glimpse running at the edge of the abbey ruins — but Liz broke to the left, back towards the wood they had just left, and Sven broke to the right. Before they could realize their mistake and come together again, the cat-dogs had run between them. Liz shone the torch at them, and the light glared red and green in their eyes, but they didn't freeze and they didn't run away. Two of them turned towards her, jogging lightly, red tongues hanging out over white teeth, and although they weren't big, she knew they were strong and she knew they would bite.

She ran forward, rattling over the loose chippings, jumping the walls and crashing down into the chippings on the other side. She could hear the holy well just ahead. From behind her, from the sanctuary of the abbey, she heard a man's cry.

"Sven!" She spun, and the light of her torch spun with her, lighting fans of leaves, trunks, a wall. Back and forth she sent the beam, at the same time turning her head constantly as she watched for cat-dogs near her. There seemed to be none. They seemed to have gone, left her. But something was moving out there in the abbey. She could hear the shifting of the stone chippings as something moved in them. "Sven!" Still no answer.

She scrambled up the bank from the ruins and gained the clear path. At her feet trickled the holy well. She shone the torch forward and saw the path lead into a dark tunnel of leaves and trunks: the path to the farm. She started for it — and a cat-dog frisked before her. It snapped its teeth at her, playful as a puppy, and in the light of the torch, its teeth and muzzle were stained dark.

She took a step or two backwards, and would have turned and run unthinkingly back along the path into the wood, but a soft bark made her turn and swing the light. Another cat-dog was behind her.

Sheer terror gave her the courage to run forward on the path home, swinging the torch at the cat-dog that blocked her way. The animal dodged the blow neatly and then, with a dancing step, darted in and drove its teeth into her forearm.

She couldn't believe it, and tried to pull her arm back as if nothing had happened. The weight dragging down on her arm was greater than she could ever have guessed, and not a dead weight, but an active, strong weight, trying to pull her down. Her flesh was tearing. She dropped the torch. Another tug from her other side — the other cat-dog had hold of her jacket. From somewhere close by came an eager yip as the others hurried to join the attack.

She clenched her free fist, and banged the

cat-dog that held her arm on the nose. The blow jarred the teeth in her wound and it must have hurt her as much as she hurt the cat-dog, but she punched again and the clamped teeth released their hold.

She was away, running, leaping from the path and crunching down in the loose chipping of the abbey. At first a weight hung on her — the cat-dog that had seized hold of her jacket — but then it fell away and she bounded forward.

She had no light now and couldn't see where she was running. When she sprang, she couldn't see where she might land. In the fitful, overcast moonlight, the low walls were a dense black, the beds of stone chippings a paler grey. She didn't know if the cat-dogs were still after her; she couldn't hear them.

Her shin cracked against a stone, and she catapulted forward over the wall and went sprawling noisily and painfully in the chippings. Her teeth clashed together, nipping her tongue and filling her mouth with blood and pain. For one second she lay still, winded; but then a slight pattering sent her struggling forward again, swimming in the chippings, panting for breath.

She bumped into something that was hard and yet yielding, that rolled a little with her impact, and sighed. She felt cotton under her fingers and a faint warmth. A smell — not the smell of damp woodland earth. Aftershave. She had found Sven.

She grasped a handful of his shirt and shook him. His body moved slightly, heavily, but he didn't move or make any sound. "Sven," she said. "Sven." Her hand found his face, his nose, her fingers slipped into his mouth. He didn't move. Her hand moved to his chin, and his head tipped sideways — and, slipping lower, her fingers found another, wet mouth. She snatched her hand back, feeling the wetness turn sticky and thick, as only one liquid did. Sven might have sighed, but only because she had fallen on his chest.

For a moment, she was stunned. Then she saw a blackness slip along the top of a black wall, and there was a little run of yips, like laughter. The skoffins scoffing.

Dad's gone, she thought. Sven's gone. I'm on my own.

All the foxes, she thought, all over the country . . . in the towns . . . dens in back-gardens, eating take-away food from litter bins. And all the cats, in every street, pet cats. Who knew how many skoffins, everywhere, cunning as foxes, curious as cats, very clever and very fierce.

The darkness moved in front of her and she kicked out at it and yelled. A nip came at her arm — a quick, bruising, testing nip, which she shook off.

People will take them for foxes — "How sweet, I'll put out some scraps" — or they'll take them for cats.

Noises in the garden at night. Soft scuttering sounds of pads in the street behind, at night. A movement, low and quick, seen from the corner of the eye. It could be a fox. It might only be a cat.

She brought her feet under her, and sprang and ran. Something grabbed at her as she went by, but she was away, running, for the path to the farm, refusing to care about the pain in her leg, the burning in her bitten arm. The darkness sent her smacking into a tall section of the abbey wall. She slapped at it with her hands, seeking its edge, a way round it. A weight fastened on her ankle, and pulled. She clawed at the wall, pulled against the weight, struggling to stay on her feet. Another grip clamped about her other leg, in the calf, pulling . . . She went down.

She thought: this is it . . . this is it . . .

THE PIANO

Diane Hoh

Laura sat down on the narrow, padded red velvet bench and flexed her fingers. Her knuckles cracked.

"Laura!" From the living room across the hall came her stepmother's voice — screech of a night owl, shriek of an angry cat, hyena's howl. "I can't *hear* anything!"

Laura sent a baleful glance towards the sound. In her mind's eye she could see the tall, skinny figure with dyed red hair and pencilled eyebrows stretched out on the flowered chaise longue, one bony hand reaching out every now and then to dip into the ever-present box of chocolates. Why didn't the woman weigh a ton?

"Laura? Did you *hear* me?" Whining like an old engine. Sally-the-stepmother wasn't old — she was twenty-five years younger than Laura's late father had been. Still, she whined.

"You'll never be rich and famous like your precious grandmother if you sit on that bench like a lump. Let's get those fingers moving, dear!"

Laura muttered bitterly to the piano, "What does she mean, let *us?* It's only *my* fingers that spend hours and hours on these piano keys. I'm so tired, I can't think straight. Can't think at all. All Sally's fingers do all day is change TV channels and tiptoe through the chocs."

She sighed heavily, her fingers poised above the keys as she thought wistfully of the rock concert at the stadium last night. Sally had forbidden her to go. "Don't be silly," she had said, picking shreds of coconut from her teeth with a wooden toothpick. "Practise makes perfect, remember? You've got that competition coming up. If you win it, and you'd better, we'll be on our way, sweetie."

What do you mean, "we"? Laura thought angrily. I'm the one who's practically bolted to this piano bench. All I ever *do* is practise, practise, practise!

Nothing seemed real in her gloomy little world any more except the grim, dark-panelled music room, the piano, and the bench.

Everyone else had gone to the concert.

Even Susannah. Susannah Jeffries was Laura's strongest competitor in the race for a scholarship to the Academy of Music in London, the winner to be decided by the competition Sally had mentioned.

Laura was about to bring her poised hands down on the keys when they suddenly rippled up and down the scale on their own, as if to catch her attention. Then they began to play. They played a rock tune. It was "Long, Tall Sally."

Laura stared down at the keys. She hadn't touched them, yet here they were, sending her a message. Something about her stepmother . . .

"Long, Tall Sally" was quickly followed by the opening bars of "Black-Hearted Woman."

Laura clasped her hands. "Oh, you're right!" she murmured. "She *is*, she is! The blackest heart of all!"

If Sally had entered the room just then and said, "Why on earth are you talking to that piano?" Laura would have answered defiantly, "Well, why shouldn't I? I don't have anyone else to talk to. And who knows me better? Don't I spend every waking moment of my life on this bench? Shouldn't this piano know me better than anyone else? Besides, music is a language after all."

Talking to a piano wasn't so weird. She'd heard of stranger things. Like, for instance, her father marrying someone like Sally.

Hands resting in her lap, her voice soft and wounded, Laura asked the piano, "Why did he ever *marry* her?"

The piano played "Why Do Fools Fall in Love?"

Laura nodded, her long black hair bobbing gently on her shoulders. "Poor Daddy. He'd been alone so long after mother died, and Sally *was* kind of pretty when he met her. He wasn't foolish about anything else, only her. Sat right there in his leather recliner and let her spend every penny he ever had. Now he's dead and I'm stuck with her. I can't very well throw her out. This is *her* house. He left it to her."

The keys rippled again, more softly this time, "Tell Laura I Love Her."

"Oh, that's so sweet. I love you, too. I hate practising for hours every day, but that's not *your* fault."

It was true, Laura did love her piano. It was an odd-looking instrument, old and dark, with thick legs embellished with grotesque carvings of animal heads. Laura insisted that they were artistic, but secretly, she knew the piano was a monstrosity.

Ugly or not, the piano had been handed down to her from her grandmother, a world-renowned concert pianist until her sudden death at the age of thirty-four. Because of her success, she had died a wealthy young woman, leaving her money to her son, Laura's father, who was then a boy of ten.

Bad investments and Sally's voracious appetite for material things had dissipated the fortune until there was little left. They could barely keep up with the maintenance on the once-stately house, and Sally had suggested they sell the piano. "It's a gen-yoo-ine antique," she had told Laura's father. "Bring a small fortune."

But Laura had cried and her father, for once, had supported her.

A year later, shortly after her father's death, Laura's piano teacher, Dr. Lakis-Tabouli, had announced that in his opinion she had a very good chance of following in her grandmother's footsteps. From that moment on, there had been no more talk of selling the piano. Sally wasn't stupid — she knew a good thing when she saw it. So, Laura's practise schedule had been intensified until it had become so demanding, she barely had time for her schoolwork, and a social life was out of the question. She could no longer remember what fun felt like.

Sally was determined to be rich again, and Laura was the tool she intended to use.

Now the piano was telling Laura that it understood her plight, and it loved her. Well, it was nice that *someone* did. There was certainly no love lost between her and her stepmother, and Craig Nevins — the only boy she'd ever been interested in — had eyes only for Susannah Jeffries. As far as Craig was concerned, Laura was just another musical prodigy at Lakis-Tabouli's Music Academy.

Without her beloved piano, she wouldn't have anything. They understood each other, she and her grandmother's antique musical instrument.

A pleased smile creasing her pale, strained face, Laura lightly played "You Are My Sunshine."

The piano answered with "You Light Up My Life."

Laura laughed again, and her fatigue left her. She suddenly felt light-hearted, and stronger than she had in weeks.

"Laura!" The owl-screech again. "What are you doing in there? Have you forgotten that the competition is tomorrow afternoon? That Jeffries girl is going to steal that scholarship right out from under your nose if you don't stop fooling around."

Laura stuck out her tongue in the direction of the hallway. "Whoever wins this competition tomorrow," she explained to the piano, "gets to go to the Conservatory in London, all expenses paid. I'm not even sure I want to go there, but it's the only way I'm ever going to get away from *her,*" nodding towards the living room.

The keys played a quick, lively tune.

"I know that one! It's from the musical, *Oliver!* — 'I'd Do Anything.' " Laura straightened the pages of her sheet music. "Well, thanks, that's really sweet. But about the only thing you could do for me right now is get Susannah Jeffries out of my hair . . . out of my *life,* and I think that's too much to ask even of a wonderful piano like yourself. Now we'd better get to work before our black-hearted woman comes rushing in to strap my fingers to your keys."

Her shoulders no longer slumped, Laura began practising in earnest.

Sally went out to dinner with friends. After a quick sandwich in the cold, dimly lit kitchen, Laura slipped out of the house and, as she often did at twilight, went for a walk in the woods surrounding the house.

She had only gone a short distance when a figure on a huge, pale horse appeared in the distance. Long, silvery hair hung loose beneath the rider's red velvet helmet. She'd know that hair anywhere. Susannah Jeffries. Riding in *Laura's* woods! Of all the nerve.

Laura had once had a horse of her own. His name was Schubert, and she had loved him passionately, but Sally had sold him, reminding Laura coolly that she had no time for riding anyway. It had broken Laura's heart.

It wasn't fair that Susannah had her beautiful Arab and time to ride him, too. Was she *that* sure that the scholarship to London was already hers? Probably. Like everyone else at Lakis-Tabouli's academy.

Hidden by the thick woods, Laura was about to turn back to avoid Susannah when horse and rider began to cross the arched wooden footbridge spanning the brook that wound along the mossy banks far below.

That bridge won't hold them, Laura thought, leaning wearily against a huge old oak tree. It's not strong enough. But when she opened her mouth to call out a warning, no sound emerged.

She tried again. Nothing. Weird. There hadn't been anything wrong with her voice a few minutes earlier.

Horse and rider continued on across the narrow wooden bridge. It creaked a loud, pained protest as it felt the sudden weight.

Laura held her breath. Then, as she watched in horror, an agonized groan split the air as the bridge's wooden supports bent and buckled under the unaccustomed burden of horse and rider. The sound rapidly increased in strength and volume until the trees overhead shook with the force of it.

On the bridge, Susannah yanked her horse to a sudden halt. Laura could see the expression of bewilderment on her beautiful face.

Well, what did she expect? Laura thought dispassionately.

Then a staccato burst of sharp, cracking sounds echoed from the bridge as its over-loaded wooden posts bent towards each other like long-lost friends. When they had bent inward as far as their suppleness would allow, they groaned again and split in two, collapsing into the water, pulling the bridge in after them in a shower of shattered, splintered wood.

Horse and girl remained together at first, descending slowly, heavily, towards the stone-dappled creek far below.

Halfway down, the girl screamed once, a shrill, disbelieving sound that rang out through the woods like a siren. Then the two figures separated. The girl hit the water first, with a soft, surprised splash.

A second or two later, the horse, its pale coat gleaming in the last of the sun's rays, slammed, full force, on top of the figure lying prone in the creekbed.

Laura, one hand to her mouth, heard the sickening sound of bones shattering, of a skull being crushed. Then the cold, deep silence of a sudden death filled the darkening woods.

She turned and went back to the house to call an ambulance.

The next day, looking tired and wan, her dark hair hanging loosely around her still-slumped shoulders, Laura went directly from school to the Music Academy. Her fellow students were gathered in the reception area, their faces drained of colour.

Craig Nevins looked at Laura with interest. He was a tall, thin boy, with intense blue eyes and long, dark hair. "You've probably heard already," he said. "Suze is dead. I guess that makes the competition yours, hands down, so to speak."

Nona Scoppetone, crying in a corner, looked up with reddened eyes. "Craig! That's horrible! As if Laura's thinking of the competition now!"

But I am, Laura thought. That's exactly what I'm thinking of. How many times this morning had Sally said, with barely concealed satisfaction, "Well, I'm sorry about that girl, but she should have known better than to cross that bridge on a horse. It's all up to you, Laura. You can't possibly lose that competition now."

She wasn't going to lose it. She was going to win it. Even Craig knew that, or he wouldn't suddenly be looking at her as if, overnight, she had suddenly become interesting. She hadn't, of course. It was only that Susannah had, overnight, suddenly become dead.

"Drake's Woods?" Gower Bent, a fellow student, spoke up suddenly. "Isn't that near your house, Laura? That place where Susannah was killed?"

Laura nodded, but didn't volunteer the fact that she had witnessed the accident. Not that she felt guilty . . . Susannah had no business being there in the first place. What happened was her own fault, just like Sally said.

No reason to feel guilty. None at all . . .

In spite of the tragedy, the competition was held as scheduled.

Laura won.

Later that night, when Sally had gone triumphantly up the stairs to her room, Laura sat down at the piano in the chilly, darkened parlour.

"I keep waiting to feel wonderful," she told the piano quietly, "But I don't feel anything. Not a thing. I haven't felt anything in a really long time. I guess I'm just too tired."

The keys moved up and down, playing a tune Laura recognized as "Do You Want to Know a Secret?"

Laura nodded. "Of course. What is it?"

The keys moved up and down again. "London Bridge Is Falling Down."

"Oh, that's not funny," Laura scolded. "Susannah's *dead*. We can't feel happy about that."

Silence. Then, the keys played three tunes in rapid succession: "Yesterday," "Misery," and a reprise of "London Bridge Is Falling Down." After resting a moment, they broke into a rousing rendition of "Happy Days Are Here Again."

Laura sat perfectly still, shocked into silence. "Okay, so I *was* miserable yesterday," she admitted. "And maybe things *have* worked out better for me because the bridge collapsed. But . . . but Susannah's *dead*. You . . . you didn't . . . no, you couldn't have . . ."

Silence. The keys remained stubbornly still.

"I didn't . . . I didn't want her *dead*," Laura whispered, pushing slightly backwards on the bench, suddenly repelled by the nearness of the musical instrument. "I *didn't!*"

But she didn't need the piano to remind her that she'd won the competition and that Sally was pleased and would stay off her back for a while. Craig had asked her for a date this Saturday night, and Laura had said yes. Sally would surely let her go this time, as a reward.

The keys moved up and down again. "Let It Be," the piano ordered.

Laura nodded. "Susannah's death was really her own fault," she said in an emotionless voice. "She shouldn't have been in our woods, and she shouldn't have tried to take that big Arab over the footbridge."

"Let It Be," the piano repeated.

"I will," she said softly, getting up. "I will." She went to bed. And slept soundly.

By the evening of the following day, Laura's dreams about being allowed to have fun were thoroughly dashed. Sally had made it clear that winning the scholarship was only the beginning. The real goal, she insisted, was the money her stepdaughter would earn one day as a concert pianist. Only countless hours on the piano bench would accomplish that. When Laura balked, Sally reminded her of her father's earnest wish that his daughter follow in his mother's footsteps.

"It was his dream, Laura. How many times

have I got to tell you that? You let him down, and he'll haunt you for the rest of your life. You owe the man, after all he did for you."

The argument worked every time. Laura was haunted by the notion that she had somehow caused her father's death. When he was alive, she'd had more freedom, at his insistence, and the night he'd had his heart attack, she'd been dancing with Craig Nevins at a school affair. Craig hadn't asked *her* — she'd gathered up all her courage and asked *him*. But the entire time Laura was in his arms, he was watching Susannah.

So, nothing wonderful had happened to her that night. And if she'd been at home where she belonged, she could have rushed to her father's aid, brought him his nitroglycerin tablets and he would have lived. Instead she'd been making a complete fool of herself over a boy who thought she was about as attractive as the legs on her grandmother's piano.

She owed her father a lot.

So, shrouded in bitter disappointment, Laura practised, practised, practised. The irony was that, with Susannah permanently out of the picture, Craig persisted in his pursuit of her. But she had no time for him.

"It's *her*," she grumbled to the piano two weeks after Susannah's funeral. "That black-hearted woman! So greedy. All curled up on that chaise longue like a snake, counting up in her head all the money she thinks I'm going to make. Even if I do make it some day, she'll never be satisfied. She'll be on at me forever to keep practising so I can stay famous and rich. I'll never get rid of her and I'll never have any fun while she's around. Never!"

The piano responded sympathetically with a Beatles song, "We Can Work It Out."

"No, we can't," Laura responded gloomily. "I can't throw her out because this is her house, and she'll never leave. I'm her ticket to fame and fortune. That's the way she sees it."

Half an hour later, Sally entered the room carrying a tray with a glass of milk and a sandwich for Laura. Her own half-eaten sandwich was in her other hand. "I know you don't want to stop what you're doing, dear," she said, setting the tray on a small table beside the piano. "So I brought you some eats. I'm going out to dinner, but it'll be late, so I grabbed a little snack to tide me over." She took another bite of her sandwich. "You just keep practising, and I'll see you in the morning . . ."

But as she bent over the table, she gasped, and one hand flew to her throat. Her face turned red, she made choking sounds, and her eyes began to bulge.

"Sally?" Laura stood up. "What's wrong?"

The piano began playing the theme from the movie *Jaws*.

"Stop that!" Laura scolded, and turned to her stepmother. "Sally? Oh, God, you're choking! Take a sip of milk. Maybe that will help."

Sally's bony hands clawed at her throat. The red flush on her face rapidly deepened to a sickly purplish hue and her eyes bulged.

"What should I do?" Laura cried. "What should I do? She's choking to death!"

The piano played commandingly, "Let It Be."

Laura's head whirled, her eyes blazing down at the keys. "I have to help her! But I . . . I don't know how!" She began pounding Sally on the back. It didn't help.

Sally fell to her knees, hands still clawing at her throat. She reached out a pleading hand in Laura's direction.

"What?" Laura screamed. "What shall I do?"

The piano sent her a grim reminder: "Long, Tall Sally," "Misery," then, again, "Let It Be."

Laura's knees gave and she sank to the bench, her head in her hands, as her stepmother, her tongue protruding, writhed in agony at her feet.

Laura closed her eyes and made her mind go blank.

Finally, after one last, desperate thrash of limbs and a choked gasp, Sally lay still. Deathly still . . .

The triumphant chords of "Ding, Dong, the Witch Is Dead" from *The Wizard of Oz* rang out.

"Shame on you!" Laura admonished the piano. Her face was very white, her hands shaking. Several long, silent minutes passed, and then she whispered, "I can't believe it . . . I'm free . . . I'm free!"

The piano played "I'd Do Anything."

Laura whirled on the bench. "You? You didn't do this! She choked on a sandwich. You saw her. So did I. She choked on a sandwich, that's all. That's what happened."

The doctor agreed. Expressing gentle regret that Laura hadn't known enough first aid to save her stepmother's life, he took Sally away. Forever.

"It's not *my* fault no one ever taught me first aid," Laura told the piano defensively. "Someone should have shown me what to do, and no one ever did."

Because she was seventeen, Laura was allowed to continue living in the house. It was discovered that her father had set up a trust fund for his daughter when he married Sally, and that it would be payable to her upon her stepmother's death. "He *did* know what she was like," Laura confided to the piano, "and he didn't forget about me."

She hired a housekeeper and bought a small, cheap headstone for Sally's grave. One evening, when the housekeeper had gone home, Laura went into the music room and sat down on the red velvet piano bench. "Maybe I'll go to the Conservatory and maybe I won't," she announced. "Right now, I just want to have fun! Craig and I are double-dating tonight with Nona and Gower, and tomorrow night we're all going to a concert in the city. On Monday,

Nona and I are going shopping for a whole new wardrobe of clothes to wear to all the new places I'm going."

When the piano made no response, Laura continued, "Oh, everything's going to be so different now! So much better, so much more fun!" Her fingers rippled across the keys, playing an old song, "The Times They Are A-Changin'." She was smiling.

The keys moved slowly. "Tell Laura I Love Her," they played.

"Oh, I love you too, silly! And I'll get back to playing again. I will, I promise. But not just now. There are too many other fun things to do. I'll keep you tuned, though. There's this nice man in the village Dr. Lakis-Tabouli told me about. He'll come in every so often to make sure you're not getting rusty."

She patted the keyboard and was about to get up when the keys played plaintively an old love song, "Don't Ever Leave Me." Laura recognized the tune. It had been one of her mother's favourites.

She frowned. "Well, you didn't think I was going to keep practising now that Sally's dead, did you? Why should I?"

The keys begged again, "Don't Ever Leave Me."

Laura's frown deepened. "Look, I've spent most of the last ten years on this stupid bench, and lately I've had to practise until I thought my fingers would fall off! I'm seventeen years old and this is my chance to have fun. I'm going to take it. You'll just have to wait for me, that's all."

After a moment or two, the piano played sullenly, "What I Did for Love."

"I know," Laura said, contrite. "And I'm grateful. But did you really think that with Sally gone I'd keep up that horrendous schedule?"

"I Should Have Known Better," the piano played mournfully, regretfully.

"Yes, you should have," Laura said crisply. "Now, I've got to go. I don't want to keep Craig waiting."

But before she could stand up, the keys burst into a wild, chaotic rendition of "You Belong to Me."

"Well, I most certainly do *not*," Laura said coolly. "I belong to *me* now, for the first time in my life!"

She wasn't at all prepared for what happened next.

The piano began playing the *Jaws* theme again and, as it did, it suddenly slid forward, ramming into the piano bench where Laura sat. Then, before she could move, it gathered speed and raced across the hardwood floor, driving bench and passenger backwards until they slammed into the far wall, pinning Laura firmly between the wall and its solid, immovable bulk.

"What are you doing?" Laura screamed. "Let me out of here!"

The keys flew frantically. "Don't Ever Leave Me," it played, and then, before Laura could respond, "We've Only Just Begun."

"No!" she cried, pushing against the piano, which failed to budge. "No, we *haven't* only just begun. I'm finished with all of this. I hated it, I hated every minute of it . . . the hours and hours of practise, cooped up in this gloomy old house, no one to talk to but a stupid musical instrument, no friends, no fun . . . I *hated* it! I'm *glad* it's over, do you hear me, I'm glad!"

"Don't Be Cruel," the keys admonished coldly.

"I'm sorry," Laura whispered. She strained backwards on the bench, then pushed forwards against the piano, trying desperately to free herself. In vain — she was trapped.

The doorbell rang.

"Please!" Laura begged. "Please let me out of here. That's Craig. Don't ruin this for me, please. I promise I'll come back and play later. I will."

The huge, dark instrument remained firmly in place, playing cynically, "What Kind of Fool Am I?"

"Let me *out!*" Laura sobbed. "Let me out, *please!*"

The doorbell continued to ring, the chimes pealing shrilly through the big old house.

On the front porch, Craig Nevins finally shook his head in disgust. "Should've known better," he said angrily to Nona and Gower. "Gorgeous or not, that girl's as nutty as that grandmother of hers was. Shut up in there with that precious piano of hers! I can hear her playing. She probably forgot all about our plans."

"You must have heard the same story I heard," Nona said as they turned and made their way down the steep, wooden steps from the house. "My mother said Laura's grandmother died sitting at that piano."

"*I* heard," Craig said, "that Laura's grandmother bought that ugly old thing from some Hungarian gypsy. My dad said she never used another piano after that. Took that one all over the world with her, like it was a pet or one of her kids. Weird!"

Nona nodded. "It *is* weird. No one knew what really happened. She was rich and famous and happily married to some duke in Europe, and she had a little boy, Laura's father. She had announced that she was going to retire, to devote herself to her family. After she played her last public concert, she came home and went into her music room, supposedly to relax before going to bed. But she never came out."

"I heard the same story," Craig said. "My dad said her husband was away on business and the servants didn't know what to do. She never left that piano bench to eat or sleep or even have a bath. Her husband broke the door down when he finally got back home."

Nona shuddered. "He found her there, dead. Her fingers were just bloody stumps. She'd been playing non-stop that whole time, four or five days. Can you imagine what she must have looked like? Creepy! Maybe she *was* rich and famous, but you're right, Craig, she must have been really crazy. It's probably hereditary."

Shuddering again, Nona hurried her steps. Her companions did the same.

In the music room, a trapped Laura heard their footsteps departing. She moaned softly and covered her face with her hands, crying quietly.

The black and white keys moved up and down and the cheerful strains of "Happy Days Are Here Again" filled the room.

Laura sat up straight, wiping her eyes. Her mouth was set in a grim, straight line. "No!" she cried. "No, it's not going to be like this. I know about my grandmother. *You* did that, didn't you? I know you did! She was going to retire, and you couldn't stand that."

The piano played "What I Did for Love."

"Love?" Laura shrieked. "That's not love! And you're not going to do to me what you did to her."

Laura was small and very thin. She tilted the stool beneath her backwards, clearing a narrow space between it and the piano. Then she slid forward, legs first, until she was underneath the instrument, dropping to her hands and knees when she landed on the floor.

Above her, the keys thundered in rage, "Don't Ever Leave Me!"

Laura ignored the frightening sound. She crept to the open space between one hideous leg and the lower front of the piano. It was large enough to crawl through.

But as she slid her upper body forward into the opening, the ugly, miniature animal heads carved in the wooden leg began to pulsate with sudden life. Their shapes shifted, swelled and stretched small mouths, and then tiny sharp teeth began to nip at Laura's neck and shoulder, tearing her blouse and digging into her flesh. The cuts were small but painful.

Laura screamed but didn't stop. Sobbing softly, she pressed onward, squeezing through the opening as the cruel teeth bit at the right side of her body, her chest, her waist, her hips and thighs, drawing blood repeatedly.

Above her, the music built to a terrifying crescendo as Laura fell through the opening onto the floor and scrambled to freedom. Her right side, from neck to ankle, was dotted with vivid red polka-dots of blood.

"You're *evil!*" she screamed, backing rapidly away from the piano until she was up against the door. She sagged against it, breathing hard. "Maybe my grandmother didn't know it until too late, but *I* know it!"

The tiny heads stopped moving, shrank back into their proper positions, and fell still. The keys were silent.

Turning, Laura ran to the cellar. Finding what she wanted, she raced back up the steps and into the parlour. Her eyes blazed with fury, her hair flew around her face, her mouth was set with determination as she set about her task.

With the first blow of the axe, the piano shuddered violently, but it remained silent through the second and third blows and the two dozen that followed. Finally Laura was surrounded by a pile of splintered dark wood and ebony and ivory keys scattered about on the floor.

Exhausted, sobbing softly, Laura dropped the axe and ran from the room and out of the house. She hurried down the steps, intent on catching up with her friends, and never looked back.

Behind her, in the parlour of the old, dark house, there was a long silence.

Then, faintly at first, a gentle tinkling began,

like a tiny bell being rung. It was an infant sound, but it grew quickly, gathering strength and volume until the music room filled with a rich, promising melody. As it played, the splintered wood began to move, moulding itself back together again, then flying up into the air to attach itself to what was left of the piano frame. When all the wood was back in place, the ebony and ivory keys wafted up from the floor and settled with satisfaction into their rightful places on the keyboard.

The tune the piano played as it reshaped itself was from a musical about a little girl with red curly hair. The song spoke of a brighter future, a promise of better things to come.

But there was no promise of a brighter future in the piano's rendition; no promise of brighter days to come, of a sun peeping out from behind a cloud; no cheery, optimistic outlook.

Instead, in the icily evil notes, there was a promise of retribution, of a score to be evened, of revenge. Not tonight, but soon. Very soon.

"Tomorrow," the newly restored piano thundered, "Tomorrow . . ."

THE DEVILS FOOTPRINTS

Malcolm Rose

THE PRAYERS OF THOUSANDS OF CHILDREN IN Devon had been answered. After years without snow, the Christmas of 2004 was as white as a greeting card. By New Year, the snow had not been reduced to dirty grey slush as expected, but had packed down hard. Devon had been transformed into a giant ice rink and there was no sign of a thaw.

By the end of January, the arctic conditions had become tiresome. Then, in February, something remarkable happened. The cold winter turned even colder and the River Exe froze solid as glass. Briefly, the fascination with the extraordinary weather returned. Adventurous hikers walked right across the frozen estuary from Starcross to Exmouth and children wrapped up warm and skated on the thick ice. Yet when night came, it seemed that life had been suspended. Birds had flown south, pets and farm animals were kept indoors and hibernating creatures slept on. And it was on the night of 8th February that life became impossible. That night, it became clear who had answered all those prayers . . .

Darren was holding a party at his house. He had left the front door unlocked so that his friends could walk straight in, but even so, out of habit, many rang the doorbell and waited to be invited in from the cold. As always on such occasions Jaz and Sam were last to arrive so, despite their disguises, Darren knew straight away who they were. He found them on the doorstep, dressed as Batman and a decidedly female Robin, stamping to get snow off their boots and to keep their feet above absolute zero.

"Hey!" Jaz chimed. "That's what I call going to extremes."

"What is?"

He pointed to tracks in the snow leading up the drive to Darren's house. "Someone's come as . . . what? . . . a donkey or a goat or something. And even put the right footwear on. Look!"

In the snow were clear imprints of a foot or hoof. They were about the size of a donkey's, some ten centimetres by six, but with five or six claw marks, and had clearly been made by a two-legged creature, not an animal on all fours. Darren knew that it must be one of the guests at his fancy dress party because the footprints led up to his front door but none led away again. Besides, how else could they be explained?

"Wicked," he remarked.

"Ah, well. *You'll* be able to get to the bottom of it," Jaz said.

"How do you mean?"

"Being Sherlock Holmes for the night. You should be able to suss out who's the goat."

"Look, I know it's fascinating standing out here analysing footprints," Sam said, feigning irritation, "but can we come in before the frost-bite sets in?"

Darren laughed and stood to one side. "Sure. Come on in. The party's been up and running for some time. You've got some catching up to do."

As they edged past him, Jaz said, "Actually, I think it's a bit warmer."

"The Exe is still frozen," Sam reminded him.

"I mean the breeze," Jaz declared.

Darren breathed in deeply then coughed. "I see what you mean. It's changed direction. It *is* a bit warmer."

Sam snorted theatrically. "Bet we won't be going home in T-shirts and sandals!" she teased.

Darren's parties were always different. The standard fare of food, noise, and dance wasn't sufficient for him: there had to be an added ingredient. In the past he'd organized swimming-pool parties in the garden, a post-nuclear holocaust party when everyone turned up as diseased mutants in rags (otherwise known as the most disgusting party ever held in Dawlish), and some bizarre virtual reality computer parties. Silly, but fun. Darren's were *the* events to be seen at — even if in disguise. Something of a practical joker, he had all the qualities of a lovable rogue and his reputation for holding the best parties was aided by having a big house and generous and understanding parents who went out a lot themselves.

On the evening of 8th February, Darren's parents had braved the weather to go to a do at the Ahriman factory to mark some anniversary of its founding. Darren had been invited as well but could not bear the thought of being dragged into adult celebrations. Unwilling to miss out on a party, though, he'd persuaded his mum and dad once again to let him hold his festivities at home while they were out. They'd agreed on the understanding that this time, when they returned, there would not be any dubious foreign objects in the swimming pool or punch spilled into the computer control pads.

Inside the house, Brian was in control of the lighting, heating, music and lasers. Guests were chatting, giggling, dancing. Two brothers who collected defunct computer games had come as Super Mario (a plumber with an outlandish moustache), and Sonic (a comical sort of hedgehog), and spent the whole evening arguing and fighting. The gorgeous Kelly was so unconventional and individual that she had come as herself. She was wearing a simple low-cut white dress, guaranteed to attract as much attention as the more exotic costumes on show and to stand out in strobe or laser lights. Several of Darren's friends had masks or hoods so he was not sure who was who. In the lounge, there was no sign of half a donkey or an upright goat. With lasers flashing and revolving, he couldn't see the revellers' footwear. No one seemed to be dancing as clumsily as would a party-goer on hooves, with the exception of a scuba diver who was already regretting his decision to turn up in flippers.

"Food and drinks through in the dining room!" Darren shouted to Jaz and Sam. "Follow me!" He made his way through the dancers and out into the relative quiet of the next room. A hooded monk and a fairy were sprawled on the sofa together, kissing and oblivious to the commotion around them.

Darren pointed to the bar and said, "Help yourselves to what you want."

Suddenly, Brian's stilted voice warned, "Darren, beware. There is a noxious substance in the room."

"What?"

"You are holding a twelve per cent solution of a restricted substance, ethanol, commonly called alcohol. If drunk, it will alter your perceptions, cause dizziness and nausea. It will dehydrate . . ."

"Okay, okay," Darren retorted. "Mum and Dad's idea of a joke to programme you to say that, no doubt."

If it had not been the household computer he was talking to, Darren could have sworn that he heard Brian give the exasperated grunt of someone whose advice has been scorned.

Jaz gulped down a soda, smacked his lips and then asked, "Why call it Brian anyway?"

"I used to call him . . ."

"*It*, Darren," Jaz said. "Not *him*. It's just a computer."

"Yeah, but *it* could be anything. Brian's almost one of the family. We used to call him Mega-Brain but his new software was a bit dodgy at first. Quite a few bugs. So I renamed him Nearly Brain. And that's Brian. Right? It stuck."

Batman groaned, then, with Robin, went to join the crowds lounging in the kitchen and on the staircase. Darren swallowed some more punch and went to look for Kelly. Actually, it was easy to ask her to dance. It was the next step that was troublesome.

In mid-gyration, he manoeuvred close to her so that he could yell into her ear, "Enjoying it?"

"Yes," she yelled back above the music. "Great fun."

Darren beamed. So far, so good, he thought.

Kelly's parents had just moved to the area

so she was the new girl at school. Integration
had not been a problem for her, though. The
girls were curious about her so they mixed
almost immediately and the only problem she
had with boys was how to keep them at bay.
There was always a queue, each wanting to
be the first to bear the enviable label of Kelly's
boyfriend. Besides, most of Darren's friends
agreed that she would not have been too per-
turbed if she had failed to mix. She was in-
dependent, cultivated a willful image, and
enjoyed retaining her mystery. At the party,
she did not seem at all bothered that she was
the odd one out. Rather, she was revelling in
the attention she was attracting as the only
sensibly dressed guest.

Darren's cheek brushed against her hair as
he spoke into her ear, "Drinks in the dining
room, you know. Help yourself."

"Thanks," she replied, but carried on dancing.

"Later on, when most people have gone
home, a select few will stop on to have coffee,"
Darren added. "People like Jaz and Sam —
they're here as Batman and Robin. Maybe
we'll get in a curry if we feel like it."

"Really?" she responded noncommittally.

He wanted to issue a direct invitation but he ducked it. After all, he wasn't getting much encouragement. For the moment Kelly remained playfully aloof, but at least she hadn't told him where to get off.

They danced together until Darren needed to sluice his aching throat. "Going for a drink," he croaked in a brief pause between songs. "Want one? I'll show you where, if you like." He was hoping to have her to himself somewhere quiet — at least for a while.

Kelly didn't rise to the bait. "No, thanks. I'm okay at the moment." She smiled fondly at him but showed no sign of wanting to accompany him, and was immediately whisked away by a vampire with convincingly bloodshot eyes.

Back at the bar, Darren realized that his own eyes were sore as well. He put it down to the acrid atmosphere. Even the monk in the corner had broken away from his amorous clinch to wheeze and cough. "Brian, turn up the air-conditioning," Darren said. "It's getting a bit stale in here."

Brian's video cameras scanned each room of the house and Brian responded, "True. I detect one person vomiting in the cloakroom,

and signs of increased heart-rates and short-
ness of breath in several other guests. I have
adjusted air flow accordingly."

"I'm not sure that's all due to the atmosphere," Darren responded, grinning wryly. It
wasn't the first time he'd spent hours organ-
izing drinks and titbits for a party, only for his
friends to turn it into waste in a matter of
minutes.

"Alcohol," Brian commented drily. "I told
you so."

"Sometimes you sound just like Dad," Darren retorted. He looked round and caught sight
of the furry back of some outfit he'd not seen
before. It was supposed to be some wild creature, no doubt — possibly the one responsible
for the hoof marks on the drive. He called for
him — or her — but was too late. The figure
had slid into the darkened lounge. He went to
the same door and watched the dancers for a
while but could not make out the mysterious
guest, who had blended into the darkness.

The vampire brushed past Darren, declar-
ing, "Great party!"

"Thanks, Have you seen Kelly?"

"Yeah. Just stopped strutting my stuff with
her. Some chap in an animal mask took over."

"Yeah? What sort of animal mask?"

"I don't know. Sort of goatish. Pretty evil looking. I was impressed," he said, his fangs glinting in the laser beams. "And now, could you point me in the direction of your supply of aspirins?"

"What's the matter?" Darren asked.

"Headache," the vampire replied. "You know: pounding music, flashing lights, a touch of booze, dancing with a good woman and all that."

"Upstairs," Darren said. "Bathroom cabinet." He hesitated, then added, "I'll take you."

They pushed their way past the cluster of people on the stairs and someone shouted, "Watch him, Sherlock! Hope you've got a cross for protection."

Another guest, holding up a slice of bread, cried, "You can take my garlic bread if you think it'll help."

"I've already checked him out with holy water in front of a mirror," Darren replied. "I could see his reflection and he didn't burn up. Must be a friendly vampire, though I admit he's a pain in the neck."

Pointing out the bathroom Darren slipped quietly into his own bedroom, which was off limits to the party-goers. Except for one, of course, but right now that seemed to be just wishful thinking. He sat down in front of a computer screen and ordered, "On."

"Yes?" Brian replied at once.

"You know Kelly, do you?" he asked. "You could recognize her?"

"Yes. You danced with her earlier. She is wearing a colourless dress."

"That's right," Darren said. "Who's she with now?"

"Scanning," Brian responded. Several seconds later, he reported. "She must be in the lounge. She is not in any other room. I cannot scan accurately in the lounge because of the level of lighting."

Darren nodded, then said, "Turn up the lights just enough to show me on screen the people dancing. So we can pick her out."

The screen came to life, showing swirling lights and swirling people. The video scanned across the room, then zoomed in on Kelly.

"She is dancing on her own," Brian reported.

Darren shook his head. "No one dances on their own at my parties. Especially not Kelly. She's too much in demand. Too good-looking."

The camera panned all around her. "I confirm that she is alone," Brian concluded.

"So I see," Darren agreed. "But I can't believe it."

"Anything else?" Brian prompted.

"No . . . Er, yes," Darren replied. "Scan for someone dressed as a goat."

After a few moments, Brian responded. "There is no such person in the house."

Puzzled, Darren said, "Check again."

"All rooms checked. I confirm that there is no one matching, even remotely, my library entry of a goat."

"Forget the body, then — just concentrate on the head. Has anyone got a goat-type mask?"

"Scanning." Fifteen seconds later, Brian announced, "Negative."

Darren shrugged and sighed. "Okay. That's all."

The screen died, becoming dull green again.

Darren was beginning to lose some of his appetite for the party. There was something peculiar about it. Not just the choking atmosphere, the disappearing goat, and his separation from Kelly. Normally at parties he didn't have a worry in the world. He would immerse himself in the revelries and let tomorrow take care of itself. This time, though, he'd begun to feel a responsibility for the events and for his guests. "Bad news," he mumbled to himself and tried once more to enter into the spirit of things.

He went downstairs and danced for a while with the female Robin before handing her back to her faithful Batman. While the three of them helped themselves to crisps, peanuts and drink, Sam complained to Jaz, "Yeah, Darren danced with me all right. I should feel privileged, but his eyes were all over the place. Not on me."

"Ah," Jaz replied knowingly. "Looking out for Kelly, I bet. Like all the lads."

"No . . ." Darren began, but thought better of the denial. "Well, yes. I guess so."

"And why not?" Sam responded. "It's your party. Everyone loves your dos. Including the lovely Kelly if tonight's anything to go by. Might as well make the most of it. You stand a good chance with her tonight."

"Actually, you'll be interested to know she was last seen with a goat."

"Ah! He of the amazing footprints. Did you see him?"

"No. Neither did Brian. He seems . . . elusive."

"That's odd," Jaz replied.

"Look on the bright side, Darren," Sam said. "If it's a choice between a goat and Sherlock Holmes, I know I'd choose the great detective. Bet Kelly will too."

Darren smiled at her. "Yeah. Maybe."

He cavorted on the dance floor with three other girls — assuming that the highwayman was in fact female — but his mind was elsewhere. Kelly was nowhere to be seen. He tried hard not to imagine what she might be doing with the goat.

Back in the dining room Darren fended off Sinead, who'd been after him for weeks but who had a tenth of Kelly's magnetism, and joined the unattached lads accumulating by the bar. "Great punch," the vampire enthused.

"Yeah. Instant liquid headache," the scuba diver wheezed. "What did you put in it?"

"This and that. A bit of everything."

The boys gulped it down to show that they were real men. "I've cut out the middle man," the vampire told them. "Dissolved aspirin in mine!"

While the others laughed, Darren glanced

out into the hall and just caught sight of Kelly
trudging slowly up the stairs. The smile on his
face soon faded when he saw that the goat was
by her side. He seemed to glide without effort
while the girl looked weary. The goat helped
her up with an arm around her waist. The arm
was covered in some sort of animal fur. A tail
dangled between its legs. Kelly did not look
back but the victorious goat turned and
seemed to sneer at Darren. The face, Darren
had to admit, was brilliantly done. It looked
hairy and evil, with two small horns pointing
out from the forehead. The mask must have
taken ages to make. Crestfallen and not a little
annoyed, he spun round and headed back to
the punch.

As he poured himself a large draught of the
red liquid, Brian began to preach again. "Darren, beware. There is a noxious substance in
the room."

"Oh, don't start that again. Heard it before,"
he snapped. "You must have a malfunction.
Some of those bugs didn't get sorted out."

"But . . ." the computer objected.

"Shut up!" Darren interrupted. "That's an
order. I'm going to clear my head with a breath
of fresh air," he announced.

The cold hit him like a sledgehammer. Coming out of the warm brash interior and into the austere winter was like stepping from one world into an alien one. In the new world, his breath condensed into thick cloud and the sweat on his arms and brow seemed to freeze against his skin. Overhead, white vaporous fingers reached across the sky as if low-flying jet aeroplanes had crisscrossed the heavens. The air was suddenly sharp, almost tangy. It wasn't as refreshing as he'd hoped, and the shock of the outdoors failed to lessen his disappointment over Kelly. In fact the footprints in the drive reminded him of his failure.

He bent down and examined them closely by the light of the front porch. He wasn't sure exactly what impression a goat would leave in the snow but they looked elaborate and authentic. The only mystery was why the visitor had bothered with claws. Shaking his head, he stood up again, shivered, and went back inside.

He went directly to his bedroom and shut the door to isolate himself from the party. Activating Brian again, he described the footprints in the snow and requested a pattern recognition search.

It only took half a minute before Brian reported, "No successful match with library entries in my encyclopaedia."

"Mmm." Darren considered for a moment. "Try a wider search."

"How wide?"

"All your memory."

"A complete search will take two minutes and fifteen seconds."

"I can wait," Darren replied.

For two minutes and fifteen seconds, Darren tortured himself with thoughts of the goat and his favourite guest. It was tough, contemplating defeat by someone in a gruesome goat mask. If he couldn't win even when the opposition dressed up ugly, when could he win? He was curious about who was under the animal outfit. If the computer could identify what the hooves were supposed to represent, he might learn a little more about the person walking on them.

Before Brian revealed his findings, he said, "Search complete. One match found. Strange."

"You're just supposed to report, not come to a judgement," Darren murmured.

"I could claim that I found the source of the information strange — an old newspaper article — but I confess that my interpretation of the data arouses curiosity also. I think that you will find the article . . . stimulating."

"Let me see," Darren replied.

His screen filled with a story from the *London Illustrated News* of 24th February, 1855. With an increasing sense of bewilderment and horror, Darren read the article.

On the morning of Friday 9 February the good folk of the Exe estuary rose to find the frozen ground of their villages and towns covered with strange footprints that had not been witnessed on the previous day. The marks which appeared on the snow to all appearances were the perfect impression of a donkey's hoof — the length of four inches by two and a quarter inches; but instead of progressing as that animal would have done, feet right and left, it appeared that foot had followed foot, in a single line; the distance from each tread being eight inches — the footprints in every parish being exactly the same size and the steps the same length! The print of the small hoof also bore the marks of claws. This mysterious visitor only passed once in a straight line across each garden or courtyard, and did so in nearly all the houses in many parts of several towns and in the farms thereabouts; this regular track passing in some instances over the roofs of houses and hayricks, and very high walls (one fourteen feet high), without displacing the snow on either side or altering the distance between the feet, and passing on as if the wall had not been any impediment. The gardens with high fences or walls, and gates locked, were equally visited as those open and unprotected. Now, when we consider the distance that must have been gone over to have left these marks in a single night — I may say in almost every garden, on doorsteps, through the extensive woods of Luscombe, upon commons, in enclosures and farms, in Teignmouth, Dawlish, Exmouth and all places thereabouts — the actual progress must have exceeded a hundred miles. In fear of an unknown wild beast, servants would not go out after dark but tradesmen did arm themselves with guns and bludgeons and spent the day tracing the footsteps; but nothing was found.

It is very easy for people to laugh at these appearances, and account for them in an idle way. At present no satisfactory solution has been given. No known animal could have traversed this extent of country in one night, besides having to cross a frozen estuary of the sea two miles broad. This mystery comes in addition to the severe winter blighting the people of Devon. Supplies of bread having failed to reach them, riots have spread and many are dying through the cold and hunger. Truly, the people of Devon believe that they have been visited by Satan himself.

Darren finished reading and sat in silence for a few moments. Then he asked Brian, "Let's get this straight. Are we talking the infamous cloven hoof here?"

"Confirmed."

Only one word occupied Darren's mind. "No!" In this day and age, no one believed in visitations by the Devil. "Surely not." One hundred and fifty years ago, maybe. But not now. It just didn't make sense. But while he couldn't believe in the Satan theory, his curiosity was aroused and his alter ego, Sherlock Holmes, took over.

"Brian," he said, "you were right. It *is* strange. I think we need to get a closer look at our goat friend with the funny hooves."

"There is no such person in the house."

"Ah, yes," Darren said, recalling the computer's earlier failed attempts to locate him. "Well, I think I can prove to you that he's here."

"Yes?"

"Play back your video surveillance of the stairs. Run it fast forward from, say, twenty minutes ago."

In a matter of seconds the newspaper article was replaced on the screen by a view of the stairwell. The usual bunch of lads were congregated at the bottom, talking and drinking in comically quick time, like ludicrous silent film stars. First, Super Mario charged up the stairs, looking very green and with a hand clamped over his mouth. Then, arms wrapped around each other, the monk and the fairy padded up and past the camera, presumably to find somewhere more private. Shortly after, Kelly appeared at the bottom step.

"Slow to normal," Darren ordered.

In contrast to her usual stunning appearance, Kelly now looked awful. Probably nausea had struck her too. She grabbed the banister and dragged herself up the first few steps. Behind her the lads watched and giggled.

Darren stared at the screen in disbelief. Kelly was struggling up the stairs on her own. The image of a goat simply did not appear.

"Stop playback," Darren called. "This is . . ." He could not finish the sentence. No adjective seemed bizarre enough.

"Is anything wrong?" asked Brian.

"There *must* be a malfunction. This picture proves it," said Darren, clutching at the only rational explanation he could think of.

"Do you want me to check?"

"Yes. Perform a self-test."

"Confirmed. I shall be off-line for roughly four minutes," Brian advised him.

"Keep control of all the music and stuff downstairs. We mustn't let the punters down."

"Confirmed."

Darren's eyes were mesmerized by the characters, words and figures that flashed onto the screen in super-fast time, but his mind was full of doubt and trepidation. It was much more than mourning for a lost relationship. He was scared. More scared than he'd ever been before. His party was turning slowly into a nightmare that he didn't understand.

The thumping from the disco downstairs and the occasional raised voices told him that everything was normal. But it wasn't. He knew about the goat. The goat was anything but normal. He also knew that many of the guests felt lousy. His own head pounded, his eyes were stinging like crazy and he felt sick. And sometimes when he coughed, he felt vile slimy mucus rise in his throat until he thought he would choke on it. Maybe he didn't believe in a visit from the Devil, but he sensed that his party was going to hell.

Brian re-activated his voice and reported that all his systems were operating fully and properly.

"Then how do you explain the lack of a goat on the stairs with Kelly?" Darren quibbled.

"I cannot. I did not detect anything that requires explanation."

"Carry on with the videotape. Slow motion."

Kelly continued the long hard slog up the steps. Alone. No goat, gallant and gruesome.

Darren knew that only a complete idiot would believe that Satan himself had gate-crashed his party, but it did cross his mind that maybe Satan's image could not be captured on video, just as a mirror could not make an image of a vampire. If so, it explained a lot.

But what about Kelly? What had happened to her?

"Stop the tape," he cried. "Search for Kelly. Priority task. If necessary, light all the rooms to do it, but find her."

It only took a few seconds. "Bedroom five," Brian replied. "But . . ."

"Is she alone?

"As far as I can tell. But . . ."

"What?"

"I cannot detect life signs."

"You mean, she's . . ."

"I mean," the computer announced dispassionately, "she is dead."

It wasn't a pretty sight. If Kelly had been attractive in life, she wasn't in death. Sprawled inelegantly on the floor, her eyes were as red as the vampire's and her hair had lost its sheen. Some thick yellow stuff had burst from her mouth like ectoplasm. Her face was as grey and lifeless as plaster.

Shattered, Darren dashed from the bedroom in a panic and ran to get help from Sam and Jaz. He found them in the dining room picking over the savoury snacks. "Hey!" Jaz called. "You look like you've seen . . ."

"In a way, I have," Darren cried, almost choking. "Look, I need help. We've got to stop this party."

"What? Why?"

"Because of Kelly."

"Because you didn't manage to . . ."

"Because she's dead."

Batman and Robin stared at him for a moment, then laughed. "You had us going for a minute, there!"

Darren shook his head. "It's true! She's . . ." Unaccountably, he paused as the fairy staggered past on her way to the bar. He lowered his voice and continued, "She's in one of the bedrooms. And she was taken there by the . . . goat. But the goat didn't show on the video and his footprints match some in a newspaper article from eighteen fifty something. Then, they thought he was the Devil," he blurted. "It was another cold winter and . . ."

"Just a minute," Jaz interrupted. "How much punch have you had?"

More sympathetically, Sam said, "Let's take this one step at a time. First, let's find Kelly."

"Okay," Darren agreed. "I'll take you. But you won't like it. And I'm not going in again."

*   *   *

Batman and Robin's black masks seemed even blacker against their ashen faces. "You were right," Sam mumbled dismally. "It's . . . horrible. I can't . . . Poor Kelly," she cried. "And Jaz threw up on the carpet, I'm afraid."

Darren shrugged.

Once Darren had shown them Brian's evidence from the ancient newspaper and the video that lacked the image of the goat, Brian gave them more information of his own. "In the event of a death," he reported, "I am programmed to notify the authorities immediately and automatically. This I have done. I also tried to advise your parents of the situation via Ahriman's computer. The attempt failed because the factory's computer has been shut down, for a reason that I cannot comprehend."

"So are the police on their way?" asked Darren.

"The police force is not able to respond for about one hour . . ."

Indignant, Darren interrupted, "Why not?"

"I have been informed that they are dealing with many such incidents in the area." Brian continued monotonously, in a matter-of-fact voice, "No one must leave until they arrive. I have locked all doors."

"Great!" Darren uttered. "What do we do now?" He knew really, but hesitated before making the decision.

"Best to stop the party," Sam answered. "The others have got to know some time so let's get them all into the lounge and tell them what's going on."

"Including that stuff about the Devil being in the house?" Jaz pondered. He was still as white as Kelly's dress.

"Let's go easy on the Devil," Darren pleaded.

"Okay," Sam replied. "But we've got to say something about the goat at least. It looks like it's important to avoid him. We don't want any more bodies."

"That's a point," Darren said. "Where is he now? Is he locked in with us?"

Batman, Robin and Holmes stared at each other as the full implication sank in.

Brian commented, "There is no such creature in this house. The cause of . . ."

"Just because you haven't seen him," Darren growled, "doesn't mean he's not here.

Now, when we get down to the lounge, stop the music and turn up the lights."

"Confirmed," Brian replied obediently.

As the music faded and the lights went up, there was a communal groan from the guests. "What's up?" someone called.

"It's only midnight," another guest moaned.

"Yes, yes. I know," Darren shouted to address them all. "But something important's cropped up."

"Don't say someone's been murdered and now you're going to solve the crime, Sherlock," the vampire heckled.

"That's right. It's Party Cluedo," another party-goer piped up. "Trust Darren to think of that. One of us is the murderer and no one can leave till the culprit is unmasked."

"My money's on the vampire with two sharp instruments in the bedroom!"

"The scuba diver did it in the bathroom by drowning!"

"Who's dead anyway?" someone asked.

"Kelly," Darren replied. He said it in a tone so harrowed that, for a while, the banter gave way to sober silence.

In the moment of uncertainty, the vampire said, "Well, I must admit I haven't seen her for quite a bit."

"She went upstairs with the guy in the goat costume."

"The goat did it — with his horns!"

The laughter was stifled and not prolonged.

"You may be right," Darren muttered. "But not with his horns. Have any of you seen the goat recently?" he asked the assembled guests.

Sonic spoke up. "He went off with my brother."

Darren nodded unhappily. "Brian," he ordered, "find the guest dressed as . . . what?"

"Super Mario," Sonic answered. "A computer games character from ten years back." A degree of panic was noticeable in his broken voice.

"He is in the downstairs cloakroom," Brian responded.

"And . . ." Darren prompted.

"No life signs," the computer replied.

Sonic's face showed distrust. "This is a joke. A sick joke. You're going too far this time, Darren." He was desperate to disbelieve the computer.

"I can put it on screen if you wish," Brian's cold voice responded.

"I think you'd better," Darren answered. "So everyone can see it's no joke."

The large screen, until recently occupied with a succession of positive images that changed in time to the music, showed a body crumpled beside the toilet. Just like Kelly, Mario had been violently sick and was ghostly white. The only parts of his face that had any colour were around his eyes. They were exaggeratedly red. Red raw.

Maybe he fought all the time with his brother, but now Sonic dropped to his knees in anguish and burst into tears. He was consoled by a friend, appropriately dressed as a nurse.

Downcast, Jaz mumbled, "The goat *did* do it."

No one joked any more. They stood in the lounge in silence, staring at the floor, the screen or each other. In their costumes, they no longer looked silly or fantastic, merely incongruous and grotesque. Their faces —those not concealed by masks — expressed regret, fear, disgust, or . . . nothing. Some did not know how to react. They were waiting for torment to displace numbness. It would not be a long wait.

Darren sighed and said to the computer, "If there's anyone in any of the other rooms, Brian, better get them to come down here — and then tell us all about the footprints and the goat. It's better coming from you than me. No one would believe me."

The monk and the fairy were the last to gather sombrely in the lounge. When Brian had related the story about the Devil's footprints and Darren had enlarged on the activities of the goat, the girl in the fairy outfit suddenly burst into tears. "You mean, whoever he speaks to dies?"

"So it seems."

"No!" she cried.

"Why?"

"Because he spoke to me a few minutes ago, on the way to the loo," she stammered.

The guests seemed stupefied, unable to respond. The monk laid a trembling hand on the girl's shoulder.

"What did he . . . it say?" Darren asked.

"I thought he was drunk," she wailed. "Talked about his last visit here and spawning or something. Last time, with the cold, he said, he brought hunger. This time he said his breath brought death. I really thought he was just drunk," the fairy blurted. She panted for a few seconds, as if exhausted, then continued in a gurgling voice, "I smiled and walked past him. He said something about being busy, having to travel a lot." She stopped talking, with a look of surprise and then utter dismay as she realized that something inside her was horribly wrong.

She broke down in front of them. Her whole body shuddered with the force of her sobs, then she choked and began to writhe on the floor, her hands rubbing furiously at her eyes. Her body twitched unnaturally and her wings fractured and broke off. She clutched at her chest as her lungs pumped wildly. Then, suddenly, she let out a long wheeze and lay still.

Unnecessarily, Brian pronounced, "She is dead."

The fairy's death released them. Several guests screamed. Some ran for the front door but found it barred. A few, like the monk, stood mute — in shock.

Darren had forgotten how ill he felt himself. His head seemed to want to explode and his eyes were so irritated that they had half-closed. His throat and lungs burned and each breath fanned the flames inside him. But through the pain, he began to reason. Aloud, he mumbled, "The Devil visited here one hundred fifty years ago. Mum and Dad are out celebrating the founding of a firm — that was one hundred fifty years ago as well, if I remember rightly. That firm became today's pesticide factory. If the Devil spawned the old firm, then whatever it is —the Devil's breath — is coming from the pesticide factory."

"Yes," Brian answered him. "Your Devil's breath is an air-borne poison. I detected it earlier and tried to notify you. I have now sealed all windows because the police computer has just confirmed that there has been a leak of methyl isocyanate from Ahriman's. The whole area is affected. The gas escaped and condensed on cold surfaces all over the vicinity, and now the warm wind is evaporating it slowly. It is everywhere. That is why you have all been ill."

"Surely you can do something?" Darren yelled at his computer. "Something to stop us breathing it."

"I can only close the windows and reduce

the temperature to minimize the concentration of the vapour. I do not have filters for it. There are no effective measures that I can take," Brian responded emotionlessly. "Several lethal doses have settled on this house as on many others."

When the computer had delivered its bleak message, someone in the room laughed. Guffawed even.

Turning round, they saw the Devil standing behind them. No one had seen him enter the room but only Brian could deny his dreadful presence. The personification of evil, the creature's stance was roughly humanoid but the body was pure animal, with no hint of its gender. Its wide, hairy midriff gave way to bowed and twisted goat's legs that ended in hooves. The chest was matted and muscular. Its ample neck supported a long face with a straggling pointed beard. The sneering, convex mouth revealed uneven yellow teeth. Above it, there was an ugly flattened snout and upward-slanting eyes. They were deepset, angry and black. On either side of the face, fleecy ears jutted out. And from the top of its head, two curled stubby horns protruded. The creature smelled of death.

"Your talking machine is right," he jeered. "I approve of such machines. They make life easier — for you and especially for me!" Glowering at the assembled guests, with an expression which showed clearly that he found humans as repugnant as they found him, he spoke his final words. "Now," he announced contemptuously, "I breathe on you all."

As they stood transfixed, the Devil inhaled deeply. With his animal hands on his waist, he leaned towards them and let out a blast of warm stinging air from his putrid mouth, swivelling his head slowly so that the pungent clouds of evil breath enveloped them all, one by one.

When he had emptied his lungs, he breathed in again and laughed aloud. He looked with satisfaction at his work then turned, walked out of the room and passed through the locked front door as if it weren't there.

Even in the local newspapers, the story of the Devil's footprints was relegated to a few column inches on page two.

This morning, thousands of people in south Devon awoke to find their frozen roads, land

and gardens covered in marks that resembled the imprints of a goat's hoof with claws. The prints could be found on most properties in the Dawlish area but they also extended outwards, in straight lines, from Teignmouth to Exmouth on the coast and as far as Lympstone.

A spokesperson for the Meteorological Office suggested that the "footprints" could be explained by the freak current of warm air in the vicinity last night. Where the breeze came into contact with the snow, it partially melted the snow and pushed it forwards making horse-shoe shapes. The claw marks would be the result of condensation, the spokesperson explained. Blobs of water would form where the warm air current met the low ground temperature. The meteorologist failed to explain why the "footprints" were found regularly eight inches apart.

Devil

Other explanations ranged from an escaped kangaroo, thawed and refrozen cats' paw or great bustard prints, or simply practical jokers with a heated horse shoe. The similarity of the impressions to a cloven hoof gave rise *to the wildest explanation: a visit to Devon by the Devil himself. This view, probably held by many locals but not openly discussed, was given some credence by a local historian who pointed out that the Devil's footprints appeared in the area on exactly the same night in the freezing winter of 1885 when it was widely accepted that they had been visited by Satan.*

Not many read the piece. A much more important report under the headline, "Tragedy in the South West: Hundreds of Deaths," sidelined all other news items.

Yesterday a devastating tragedy hit the blighted Devon coast. A massive leak of deadly gas poured from a pesticide factory and is known to have killed over two hundred people in the Dawlish area. Many thousands of casualties were rushed by over-stretched emergency services to hospitals in Plymouth, Exeter, Taunton and even Bristol. The affected region has been designated a disaster area and quarantined. The true scale of the tragedy is yet to be assessed.

The chemical that leaked from Ahriman's

factory was methyl isocyanate. In the freezing conditions, the clouds of poisonous vapour settled on the area of Devon like a blanket. But last night there was also a warm wind. It evaporated the liquid and blew it unseen into every building, every home around Daw-lish. Nowhere was safe. Everyone touching the condensed liquid or breathing the vapour was affected to some extent. Nausea, blind-ness, headaches, skin burns, spasms and throat and lung damage were common among the casualties. In extreme cases of exposure, fatalities were a result of internal "drown-ing" — accumulation of fluid in the lungs.

Once the infernal chemical had escaped, nothing could stop it. There has been a public outcry for a total and immediate ban on this substance, which is used in the manufacture of several pesticides. Dr. Charon, a spokes-man for Ahriman, did not wish to make a full statement to the press at this time but "regretted the incident enormously." He cau-tioned against rash judgements but admitted that "at the very least, working practices would come under close scrutiny." He con-firmed that until the outcome of an inquiry is known, Ahriman has ceased its use of methyl isocyanate. A factory worker, who wished not to be named, implied that the leak had been caused by outside interference. "It is inconceivable that three failsafe devices that would normally prevent a release of the chemical in the event of an accident should all break down at the same time," she said. The worker suggested that someone might have sabotaged the controlling computer . . .

SOFTIES

Stan Nicholls

IT WAS LIKE THIS.

The boy wore a green baseball cap, blue jeans, black Nikes with white flashes and a T-shirt carrying the legend *Gravity — don't take it for granted*. The headphones of a Walkman pressed snugly against the stems of his gold-framed sunglasses.

The bear wore only a red silk ribbon tied in a floppy bow at his throat.

As they stepped off the bus at the shopping mall a breeze ruffled the bear's artificial yellow-orange fur. He wrinkled his snout and growled softly. The boy glanced at him and upped the Walkman's volume from tinny hiss to rhythmic buzz.

None of the other shoppers paid any attention.

Teenage boy and teenage bear strolled into

a record store. After browsing for a while the boy noticed a middle-aged security guard staring suspiciously at them from the other side of the sales floor. The bear saw him too, and his unblinking, black button eyes briefly flared. The guard looked away.

The pair emerged clutching plastic carrier bags, and the boy made for a rack of shirts outside an adjoining clothes shop. The bear stood to one side for a moment as he clacked the hangers, then lumbered over and tugged his arm. The boy checked his watch. Grinning, he playfully back-handed the bear's massive barrel chest.

Side by side, they set off in the direction of the town centre, the boy breaking step only to tease a fresh cassette from his hip pocket. Outside the sports complex the pavement narrowed and they had to walk single-file to make way for a woman and her Companion. The couple were deep in conversation, but the woman nodded politely at the boy before returning her attention to the pink polka dot giraffe loping along beside her.

A small bell round the giraffe's neck tinkled, the sound following boy and bear until they reached an intersection and it was drowned by traffic.

They crossed the road hand in paw.

Piers hated wedding receptions.

Hated the crowds and the din. Hated the grotesque drunks and their rambling speeches. Hated the insincere greetings exchanged by people who couldn't stand the sight of each other. And on this occasion hated being the one sent to cover the event for *The Journal.*

Admittedly, he was in a bad mood when he arrived, still smarting at Mr. T.'s refusal to come with him. These days the atmosphere always seemed tense at home and it was starting to interfere with Piers' work. Not that he was enjoying the job much right now. His editor insisted on assigning him to an endless round of fêtes, christenings, supermarket openings — anything but the story he really wanted to write. Assuming it *was* a story.

He abandoned his cardboard plate of tasteless food in the debris on the buffet table, remembering the old saying about how an angry man couldn't tell if he was eating boiled cabbage or stewed umbrella.

There was no need to stay. He had a few slurred quotes from the bridegroom, Alan Richards — a minor local celebrity since joining a second division football club — and knew he should get back to the office. But he couldn't face it yet.

A cheer went up at the far end of the hall as a group of revellers showered each other with spray from shaken lager cans. Someone started banging discordantly on the keys of an upright piano. A ragged chorus of "My Way" rose to add to the racket. Piers winced.

"Drink, sir?"

Startled, he turned. A panda holding a tray of polystyrene cups was standing behind him.

As Piers took in the ill-fitting waiter's costume he was hit by the thought that the sight was more than faintly ridiculous. And in a strange way, shaming. The notion was completely alien, but somehow heightened his feeling that there was something going on he didn't understand.

He found it impossible to meet the panda's passive gaze as he reached for an orange juice. Some of it splashed into the tray, and against the waiter's rubber palm, and he directed a mumbled apology at the Companion's departing back. Draining the cup, Piers elbowed his way to fresh air.

Outside, the sun was beginning to set. A photographer, anxious for a few last shots, fussed around the bride and groom. The bridesmaids, four dolls dressed in frothy blue gowns, golden wire wool hair piled beehive-style, giggled together in a corner. Two page-boys nibbled chunks of wedding cake on a nearby bench.

A fleeting blast of noise and light burst from the hall. A young man stepped out, blinking, his jacket draped over one shoulder. In his free hand he held a black plastic object roughly the size of a paperback. Piers instinctively patted his side pockets, found them empty and smiled sheepishly. The young man came over.

"I think this is yours."

Piers accepted the portable tape recorder, slipping its strap around his left wrist.

"Thanks. I've lost more of these than you've — "

"Been to lousy wedding receptions?"

They laughed.

"I suppose it *is* pretty gruesome?" Piers said.

"You're a journalist, aren't you?"

"Yeah." He held out his hand. "Piers Kennedy. I'm with *The Journal.*"

"Matthew Richards, Mr. Kennedy. The groom's my uncle."

"Call me Piers. Any plans to follow him into professional football, Matt?"

"No way!" He gave his jacket a shake, began putting it on. "As a matter of fact, I'd like to be a reporter."

"So I'm talking to a potential rival, am I?"

Matt flicked a strand of jet black hair from his forehead, slightly nervously Piers thought, and he regretted teasing him.

"Only kidding. But the usual advice I give anybody wanting to go into journalism is *'Don't.'* It's nowhere near as glamorous as most people think." Noting Matt's frown, he added quickly. "Mind you, that's what *I* was told. You leaving now?"

"Yes." He nodded at the hall. "I've had enough of that for one day. I'm just going to pick up my Companion. How about you?"

"Er, mine's not with me." The memory of Mr. T.'s unreasonable behaviour flooded back, along with Piers' irritation. "He had to stay at home. I'll walk over with you, though."

Naturally the Companions had a separate

hall, in this case a large, rather shabby wooden hut well away from the main building. Matt barged straight in. Piers followed, and it took him a few seconds to adjust to the gloom inside.

What he saw chilled him.

The place was full of Companions. Dolls, pandas, teddies. Grey-furred koalas, dwarf trolls with shocks of green hair, woolly gorillas. Further back, in the shadows, hulking, indistinct shapes he couldn't identify. There was nothing unusual about this. What was spooky was the *silence*. And the fact that every Companion in the room was absolutely still, like figures in a waxworks. Piers wondered if they were always like this when people weren't around. Or whether they had frozen at his and Matt's unexpected entrance, as though caught planning some mischief or conspiracy.

It was an absurd idea. At least, it would have been until recently. Now Piers wasn't so sure.

Matt seemed equally affected by the scene. He stood awkwardly in the doorway, lost for words. Piers touched his arm.

"Matt?"

"Oh. Yeah." He took a step forward and peered into the murk. "Rufus?"

For the space of three heartbeats, nothing happened. Then a bear near the front turned his huge head their way.

Very, very slowly.

As soon as he did so, all the others turned as well, just as unhurriedly. Scores of eyes regarded the humans. Cold eyes.

Piers had never felt so uncomfortable in the presence of Companions before. It was as though he had interrupted something intensely private, and was despised for it.

Matt broke the spell. "Come on, Rufus. We're going."

The bear's lips twisted into a copy of a smile. There was no warmth in it.

"Yes, Matthew. Of course." There was no emotion in the guttural voice either.

They walked to the street together. No one spoke. Before they parted, Piers wrote his telephone number on a scrap of paper and gave it to Matt. He told him to call if he wanted to talk about his ambition to be a journalist. Piers liked him, but that wasn't the only reason he did it. He guessed Matt was having a problem with Rufus. Maybe

it was similar to the one Piers had with
Mr. T.

Or perhaps both of them were trapped in
something much bigger.

At his car, fumbling for the keys, he chanced
to look up. Matt and his Companion were moving away, but the bear was staring back at
Piers over his shoulder. He wore an expression of pure, savage hatred.

Piers shuddered.

"You don't think we've overdone it with the
flowers, do you?"

"Stop *fussing*, Jerry. Everything's lovely."
Cora pointed to the chair next to her bed.
"Come and sit down. Calm yourself."

She returned her attention to their baby.
Cradled snugly, the child was sucking her
mother's little finger.

Jerry did as he was told and sat, but couldn't
stop fidgeting. For the hundredth time he
scanned the hospital room. Then his eyes
darted to the clock on the bedside table.

"They'll be here any time now."

Cora smiled and reached for his hand. "I
know, dear. And it's going to be all right. Don't
worry."

There was a double rap at the door. Jerry leapt up, nervously straightened his tie, and went to open it.

A small but impressive group shuffled in. They were led by a doctor in a white coat. Next came a smartly dressed man with a brief-case. After him, a nurse, wheeling a cot containing a bundle wrapped in a pink shawl. A doll followed, clasping a bouquet of roses. Finally, stooping slightly to avoid the top of the door frame, a bear.

The room suddenly seemed a lot smaller.

Greetings and introductions over, the cot was pushed to the end of Cora's bed and everyone formed a semi-circle.

The smartly dressed man opened a small leatherbound book, cleared his throat and began to read.

"We are gathered here to celebrate the bonding of this child . . ." he inclined his head toward the baby ". . . and this Companion . . ." a dip in the direction of the cot ". . . as friends, consorts and soulmates for as long as they both shall live."

He gently lifted the baby from Cora's arms. "Let it be known that from this day forward

Karen Grace Taylor is bound to her Companion in the eyes of the Law."

Handing the baby to the nurse, he looked down at the cot. "And that henceforth this Companion . . ." He faltered and turned to Jerry.

"Crystal," Jerry said.

". . . this Companion, Crystal," the official continued, "shall serve, support and protect her charge at all times. I declare this child and this Companion bonded." He closed the book and offered Cora and Jerry his congratulations.

A polite round of applause echoed him. But Jerry noticed that Vanda the doll and Chad the bear, his and Cora's Companions, didn't join in.

The smartly dressed man snapped open his briefcase, pulled out a sheet of paper and handed it to Jerry. "The final legal formality, Mr. Taylor," he explained.

Jerry signed the document and passed it back. It was witnessed by the nurse after she had placed the baby in the cot next to its Companion. Mr. and Mrs. Taylor thanked everyone and they all trooped out.

Alone again, they embraced. "It was wonderful," Cora said, her eyes dewy. "Karen's going to be looked after and loved by all three of us now."

In the cot, the tiny panda stirred and let out a squeaky bleat, like a young lamb. It wriggled closer to baby Karen and placed a little furry arm around her. Jerry and Cora beamed.

It was the happiest day of their lives.

It was the unhappiest day of Pier's life.

Teds could be grumpy, everybody knew that, but Mr. T.'s moods were getting him down. And what really made Piers angry was that he didn't know why he was acting this way. Hadn't he always been kind to Mr. T.? Shown him every consideration? Been there when he needed him?

The bear was out in the garden, skulking around miserably as usual, but Piers had made up his mind to confront him when he came in. This thing had to be cleared up.

The back door slammed.

Mr. T. walked into the living room and slouched on the sofa without a word. Piers was strangely uneasy in his presence, a feeling he had never had with his Companion until just a few weeks ago, when all this moodiness began. He sighed.

"Come on, what's wrong?" he asked.

No reply.

He tried again. "Look, if I've done anything to upset you, I'm sorry. Can't we talk about it? Please?"

The bear seemed to notice him for the first time. "You wouldn't understand."

"Try me."

"Have you ever wondered what it's like to be a Companion?"

Piers was surprised by the question. It didn't make sense. "What do you mean?"

"It hasn't occurred to you that I might have a mind of my own, has it? That I'm sick of always doing what you want, going where you want to go, being what you want me to be."

Even more puzzling. Companions just don't talk this way.

"You've got a good life here, haven't you?" Piers said. "I don't see the problem." It came out rather more sharply than he intended, and he could see the bear's anger rising.

"I said you wouldn't understand," Mr. T. got up and plodded to the door.

Piers reached him as he was turning the handle. He put one hand over the bear's paw, the other on his burly forearm. "Don't go. I'll try to understand, Mr. Thumpy. Just — "

"Take your filthy hands off me."

The words were quietly spoken, but filled with as much menace as if they had been bellowed. They were like a slap in the face to Piers. He let go and backed off.

The bear's eyes bore into him. His voice was higher now, more intense. "And don't you ever, *ever* call me by that stupid name again."

Piers was startled and confused. For the first time, he realized what a big, powerful creature Mr. T. was. It amazed him that he had never been aware of it before. As his life-long Companion towered over him, his face a mask of fury, Piers saw him in a totally new light. It frightened him.

Time slowed to a snail's pace as they faced each other, motionless, neither speaking.

The telephone warbled.

It snapped Piers out of his trance. He retreated clumsily, banging a low table with the back of his knees and sending a lamp flying. Ignoring it, his eyes fixed on Mr. T., he scrabbled for the receiver on his desk.

The bear remained at the door, radiating malice.

"Hello?" Piers realized his voice sounded tinny and breathless.

"Piers? Is that you?" His caller sounded pretty shaken himself.

"Who is this?"

"It's me. Matt. Matthew Richards. We met at — "

"I remember." He glanced at Mr. T. "This isn't a good time, Matt. Perhaps — "

"I need your help, Piers. Something . . . *bad's* happened to Rufus. There's nobody else I can — "

"Okay, take it easy. Give me the address." He scribbled it on the pad, tossed the pen aside. "Right. I'll be there as soon as I can."

When he got off the phone, Mr. T. had gone.

As he drove to Matt's house, Piers tried to make sense of what was happening. Mr. T. was acting completely out of character. There were the stories he'd heard about other people's Companions and *their* odd behaviour. And now Matt was having trouble with Rufus. Could all these things be connected? If so, how?

He arrived at the address he had been given in time to see two men in green overalls carrying a stretcher out of the house. Rufus, head and right arm bandaged, was lying on it, eyes closed. At the pavement end of the garden path, Matt held the gate open for them. Piers got out of the car and hurried over.

"Oh, Piers. Thanks for coming." Matt looked relieved to see him. His face was chalky white.

They watched as the stretcher was slipped into the back of the transporter. The doors were closed, revealing the words COMPANIONS RECOVERY SERVICE in large red letters, then the attendants clambered into the front seats. The van took off with siren wailing.

"I'm sorry to drag you over here, Piers, but my parents are away and — "

Piers cut him off with a wave of his hand. "It's all right. Just tell me what happened."

"Rufus was attacked."

"*Attacked?*"

"Yeah, by a gang of thugs, right here outside the house."

"How is he?"

"They say he's going to be okay. But he's pretty shaken up."

"So are you. Let's go inside and talk about this."

Sitting at the kitchen table, sipping a mug of strong, sweet tea, some of the colour returned to Matt's face.

"Now, let me get this straight," Piers said. "Rufus was beaten up by a bunch of hooligans. . . ?"

"Yes."

"How come they picked on him?"

"Can't say. He probably gave them some mouth. I always tell him to ignore those sort of idiots, but he's been really grumpy lately."

That struck a chord with Piers.

"Anyway," Matt went on, "the first I knew about it was when I heard this terrific disturbance outside. When I got out there they were running off. Mind you, they did catch one of them."

"Really?"

"Yeah. My sister, Emma, was here at the time and she called the police. They picked him up a couple of blocks away."

"Where's your sister now?"

"She went out just before you got here. Her Companion was a bit cut up about it all, you know? She's a doll, and you know what *they* can be like." He made a sour face and Piers smiled. "Emma took her for a walk."

"Do you know where the police are holding this guy?"

"Princes Street, I think."

"Good. Can I use your phone?"

Piers knew a Detective Sergeant called Hopkins at Princes Street police station. When he got there, he was surprised when Hopkins said he could see Nicholas Barker, the arrested man.

"You don't normally let journalists interview prisoners," Piers commented.

"Well," Hopkins replied, "he isn't actually a prisoner. We're not charging him."

"Why not?"

"No witnesses. He's one of the gang that had a go at that Companion. Got to be. But there's nothing we can do without proof. We're just checking if he's wanted for anything else before letting him go."

"Why should he speak to me?"

"Because you're the Press. He wants some publicity for his ideas about Companions. Really down on them, he is."

"You've no doubt Barker was involved?"

"I'm sure of it." The sergeant frowned. "We're getting more and more reports about attacks like this all the time. Some of them very serious. And as you know the most we can do these people for is damage to property. But then, assaulting a Companion's not the same as assaulting a human, is it?"

Sergeant Hopkins took Piers to an interview room and left him with the suspect.

Barker was a picture of arrogance. He sat on a chair balanced on its hind legs, his feet on the table, hands laced behind his neck.

"You're that reporter bloke, aren't you?"

"That's right, and I haven't got much time. I just want to ask you a couple of questions." Piers flipped open his notebook.

"Ask away."

"Why did you attack that Companion today?"

"You can't prove I did, and neither can the cops."

"Let me put it another way then. What do you think about him being attacked?"

Barker grinned crookedly. "Oh well, if it's an *opinion* you want, that's different. I think it served him right."

"Why?"

"I hate the parasites. Idle, they are, and stupid. Dead stupid. Makes me flesh creep, the way they slobber over you, always getting under your feet. And they smell, you know, some of 'em. Who needs it?"

"If you feel that way, how do you get on with *your* Companion?"

"Haven't got one."

Piers was shocked. He knew there were people who didn't have Companions, usually those disabled in mind or body and unable to cope, and even they were very rare. Boasting of not having a Companion was something Piers had never come across before. It was like saying you'd cut off your right arm and being proud of it. He almost felt sorry for Barker. But only almost.

"Why haven't you got a Companion?"

"Got rid of him, didn't I? Ted, he was. Useless object. Took him down the town hall and told 'em I didn't want him no more."

"What did they do with him?"

"Dunno."

"Don't you care?"

"*No!* If me and me mates had our way, there wouldn't be no Companions."

"Where would they go?"

"Search me. Dump 'em on a desert island, chuck 'em down a coal mine. Better yet, shoot the lot of 'em. They're not wanted."

"And you think it's okay to use violence against them?"

"I don't know nothing about no violence. But so what if a few Companions get a good kickin'?"

Before Piers could answer, the door opened. Sergeant Hopkins came in.

"All right, Barker, you're clear. Off you go. Don't let me see you in here again."

Barker smirked, righted his chair with a crash and kicked it aside. He thrust his hands into his trouser pockets and swaggered over to Piers. "You tell people about them dirty Companions, right? You tell 'em — "

"*Mister* Barker," Hopkins interrupted. "I suggest you do with your mouth what you've done with your mind — close it. Now, *out!*"

The Royal Infirmary for Companions was a run-down old building Piers had never visited before, and he got lost twice in the endless corridors before coming to the dormitory Rufus was in. The bear was propped up in a large iron-framework bed. Matt was sitting beside him, along with a young woman Piers didn't recognize.

Matt brightened when he saw him. "Hello, Piers. This is Emma, my sister. Emma, this is Piers, the journalist I told you about."

The girl leaned over and shook his hand. "Hi. Thanks for coming."

They all looked at Rufus.

"And how's the patient?" Piers wanted to know.

"He's fine," offered Emma.

"Oh yes, fine," Rufus said bitterly. "Insulted, beaten up on the street, treated like — "

"For goodness sake!" Matt cut in. "You're not badly hurt. And at least the police got one of them."

"Ah," said Piers. "I'm afraid they had to let him go."

Emma was outraged. *"What?"*

"No evidence, apparently."

"Surprise, surprise," Rufus grumbled. "One law for us Companions and another for you humans. As usual."

Matt was obviously embarrassed at the bear's rudeness. "Have you got time for a coffee, Piers?"

"Sure. 'Bye Emma. Nice to meet you. 'Bye Rufus. Take care."

The bear ignored him.

They didn't make it to the cafeteria. Outside the ward they bumped into a grey-haired man in a green tunic. Matt introduced him as Dr. Reynolds, the medic in charge of Rufus's case. Piers asked the doctor how many Companions were brought in after being attacked.

"Far too many, Mr. Kennedy, and the number's increasing all the time."

"How long's this been going on?"

"It started building up about a year ago, I'd say. Before that, almost every Companion we saw here had been in an accident of some sort. Just occasionally, we'd get one injured by his human during a row, but they were really unusual."

"And now?"

"Now we're seeing this kind of thing almost every week. Organized attacks. And nobody seems to be taking them seriously."

As if on cue, a trolley was wheeled past bearing a furry red chimp. Her left leg was missing.

"There's an example," Dr. Reynolds said.

"They brought her in last night. In fact, you'll have to excuse me now. I'm part of the repair team."

He trotted off to catch up with the trolley.

"You're a pain in the butt, Kennedy."

Murray Baxter, editor of *The Journal,* was not known for mincing his words. Piers, fists clenched in frustration, sat in Baxter's office and suffered the lecture in silence.

"You come in here," the boss added, "with a crazy story about Companions doing weird things and gangs of toughs roaming the streets, and expect me to believe you."

"I can prove it, chief."

"You can't. All you've got is a few comments from some sawbones and what you call a hunch. Well, let me tell you, young man — "

One of the many telephones on Baxter's vast desk rang. He snatched at it, yelled, "*Not now!*" and slammed it down again.

He carried on as though nothing had happened. "Let me tell you that when you've been in this business as many years as I have, *then* I'll start listening to your so-called hunches." He pushed his glasses back up the bridge of his nose.

"Maybe I haven't got any cast-iron proof, but something's going on, I know it."

"Really? What?" Baxter snorted.

"I think things are breaking down. Between us and the Companions, that is."

"Nonsense!" his editor roared. "Just look at me and Troy." He jerked his thumb at the ageing panda sprawled on a settee by the wall. "Fifty-eight years together and never a cross word. Isn't that right, Troy?"

"That's right, Murray, never a cross word," his Companion confirmed. "Through thick and thin," he croaked. "Good times and — "

"Thank you, Troy, that'll do," Baxter told him.

Piers thought about how some humans and their Companions grew to look and act like each other. Baxter and Troy were classic examples. He bit his lip to stop himself laughing.

Baxter brought his fist down on the desk. "Humans and Companions have always been together and always will be! It's the natural way of things and nothing's going to change it!"

"Supposing I could come up with evidence? Something you couldn't ignore?"

The editor slumped back in his chair. "Do

that, Kennedy, and I'll take you seriously. But I very much doubt you can."

Another phone rang. Baxter picked it up and barked, "Just a minute!" He put a hand over the mouthpiece. "Close the door on your way out."

Piers slammed it.

In the spacious newsroom outside, several reporters were studying some photographs. He wandered over.

"Hi, Jim, Dave. What's up?"

Jim tossed over a photograph. It showed a car that had crashed into a wall. A human arm could just be seen poking out in front of it.

"Odd one, this," Jim said. "Woman stops her car outside her house and goes to open the garage door. Leaves her Companion sitting in the passenger seat with the engine running. Next thing, the car shoots forward and crushes her."

"How?"

"There didn't seem to be a mechanical fault. Best guess is that her Companion got itself tangled with the accelerator in some way. Sad. But just one of those bizarre accidents, you know?"

"Yes," Piers said thoughtfully, "I suppose so."

The fireman wiped sweat from his forehead with the back of his arm. He leaned against the cab of the engine and clicked on the radio handset.

"Hello, sir? Yes, we've got it under control now."

He scanned the smouldering ruin. The front door of the house hung at a crazy angle, black smoke billowing from inside. A stream of water flowed over the doorstep and into the garden. Two other firemen jogged past holding a ladder.

"What?" He put a hand over one ear so he could hear better. "Yes, I'm afraid so, sir. Three deaths that we know of. Two adults and a child. Name of Taylor. Didn't stand a chance. The house is completely gutted."

An ambulance pulled away noisily, blue light flashing.

He had to shout into the microphone. "The amazing thing, sir, is that their Companions got out. Yes, not a mark on them."

He moved to allow someone to pass.

"No, they haven't a clue how it started. Say they were woken up by the fumes and just managed to escape before the place went up. Yes, they were. *Very* lucky."

He felt really sorry for the bedraggled Companions standing over by the police car. Funny, but they didn't seem to be taking it too badly. He supposed it was the shock. They looked quite pathetic though, wrapped in red blankets, their faces streaked with soot and grime.

A bear, and a doll with a baby panda in her arms.

"So that's how it stands. If I can come up with proof, my editor will give me time for some serious investigation."

"What kind of proof?" Matt asked.

"That I don't know," Piers replied gloomily.

A waitress arrived and served them with two cups of coffee. It was raining and the café was nearly empty. Piers stared through the window at the traffic crawling by outside.

Neither of them spoke for a moment. Then Matt said, "Something peculiar happened today."

"Yeah?"

"It may not mean anything, of course."

"Go on."

"When I was coming back from the infirmary with Rufus, another bear came up to us in the street. Or up to Rufus, rather. I hadn't seen him before."

"And?"

"They stood talking for a while," Matt said, "then this other bear passed something to Rufus. They didn't think I saw, but I did."

Piers began to look interested. "What was it?"

"A small piece of folded paper. Rufus scrunched it in his paw, and I didn't say anything. Then, this afternoon, I found it in the waste bin in the living room. It was torn in half and screwed up."

"Have you got it?"

"Yes." Matt put his hand in his jacket pocket. "Here it is. I taped it back together. Doesn't make much sense though."

He laid it on the table and smoothed it down. It was a perfectly ordinary-looking sheet of note paper, torn from a lined pad. All it had written on it, in blue ink, was a *12,* followed by the words *17 Gance*. Piers rested his elbows on the table, chin in palms, and studied it.

Suddenly his eyes lit up and he slapped the plastic table-top. "Got it!"

Matt was puzzled. "What do you think it means?"

"It's that word Gance. A very unusual name. There's a place down by the river called Gance Road. Suppose it's an address — 17 Gance Road?"

"And the 12?"

"That could be a time. Rufus was handed it this afternoon, right? After midday?"

"Yeah."

"So it's a time and place for — "

"A *meeting!*" they exclaimed together.

"It has to be, Matt. Let's assume it's to-night. I'm going to be there."

"Not without me, you're not," Matt told him.

They parked two streets away and walked to Gance Road. It was a rough part of town and few of the street lights were working, but a full moon lit their way.

When Matt told Piers that Rufus had slipped out of the house, thinking Matt and Emma were asleep, Piers knew they were on to something.

He looked at his watch. 11:55. They had to get a move on.

Number seventeen turned out to be an abandoned warehouse on a derelict street. A light flickered in one of the lower windows, then as quickly went out. Piers and Matt decided it would be unwise to try the front door. They crept around to the back. Matt discovered a smaller window secured only by two rotting pieces of wood.

They quietly climbed in.

A small, empty room, covered in years of dust. Piers padded over to the door and cautiously opened it. There was a corridor beyond. At the end of it, another door, which creaked noisily. Afraid someone would hear them, they waited a moment.

They were on a landing. A wooden barrier about a metre tall, faced them. Stooping, they went to it and gingerly peeped over.

The scene below took their breath away.

It was an immense cellar. Softly glowing oil lamps were scattered around the place. A makeshift platform, built from packing cases, occupied one end.

Scores of Companions of every kind, possibly a hundred or more, filled all the available space. They stood, they sat, they leaned against the shadowy walls or huddled together in groups.

And, as on the day of the wedding, they were mute and immobile.

It was so deathly quiet, Piers feared the crowd could hear his heart beating. Very carefully, he removed the lens cap from the infrared camera hanging around his neck. He lifted the camera, and looked through the viewfinder. But he didn't dare risk clicking the shutter. Then there was a flurry of movement at the front of the gathering and Piers had another shock.

Rufus walked on to the stage.

Matt's fingers dug into Piers' arm. Piers prayed he wouldn't do anything impulsive and expose them.

Rufus raised his arm and the silence was broken. A great roar went up. Piers took advantage of it and rapidly snapped half a dozen photographs.

The clamour suddenly stopped. Rufus addressed the crowd.

"Brothers and sisters! The time of our deliverance draws near!"

Another round of cheers and muffled claps from leathery paws.

"We have suffered long enough! The humans demand our love, our devotion, our obedience! What do they give us in return? Contempt! What rights do we have? The rights of property, of owned things!"

Uproar from the audience. Piers took another batch of photos.

"Are we not as they in our hearts? If they wound us with their tongues, do we not grieve? If they prick us, do we not cry out? If they cut us, does our stuffing not flow?"

He was answered with shouts of "Yes! Yes!"

"As some of you know," Rufus said, his voice lowering, "I have recently suffered at their hands myself."

A Companion yelled. "Shame!" There was a rumble of agreement.

"Yes, I suffered. And I suffered doubly. They robbed me of my dignity, and would have robbed me of my life. Yet those responsible are not to be punished."

His voice rose again. "We cannot look to our masters for justice! The only justice we

can expect is that which we take for ourselves!
Some brothers and sisters are beginning to
strike for freedom! Join them! Cast off your
chains!"

Bedlam. Companions whooped, screamed,
cheered and shrieked. They stamped their
feet, hooves and paws. A chant broke out.

*"SET US FREE! SET US FREE! SET
US FREE!!!"*

Piers used up the last of the film and tugged
at Matt's sleeve. He mouthed *Let's go* at him.
Keeping low, they moved away.

All the way back, Piers expected they would
be discovered. And if they were caught, what
then? It was an uncomfortable thought, and he
tried to push it to the back of his mind. As
they eased themselves through the window
they came in by, he noticed that Matt's hands
were trembling uncontrollably. When they finally made it to the street Piers was panting
with relief himself. Heads down, they set off
for the car as fast as they could.

Had either of them looked back, they would
have seen the door to the warehouse open.

Rufus came out. Another Companion joined
him. They watched Piers and Matt as they

turned the corner, then Rufus whispered something to the other bear.

Mr. T. nodded his head gravely.

"The important thing," Piers said as they sat in the car outside Matt's house, "is that you carry on as normal. I know that's going to be difficult, but Rufus mustn't know we suspect anything."

"Okay, I'll try. But it was incredible, Piers! All that *venom*! Rufus had been behaving badly lately, but I'd never believe . . ."

"It was a shock. I appreciate that. I just hope they're a bunch of hotheads and it isn't more widespread."

"And what was all that stuff about. 'Some brothers and sisters are beginning to strike for freedom'? What do you think he meant by that?"

"I don't know." But Piers kept thinking about the photograph he'd seen at the office and was afraid he did. "The important thing is that we've got proof." He held up the camera. "I'll get these developed for Baxter. He'll have to listen to me now."

"And the police?"

"Yes. I'll take copies round to Sergeant Hopkins. With a bit of luck, we can nip this in the bud."

"I hope you're right, Piers. I really do."

Piers had converted the spare bedroom into a dark room, and he set about developing the pictures as soon as he got in. Almost all of them came out and they were good. There was Rufus on the ramshackle stage, and shots of his frenzied audience.

He realized the photographs didn't prove any kind of evil intent in themselves, but the gathering was unusual enough to whet Baxter's curiosity. And the police would want to know what a mob of Companions were doing meeting in a cellar in the middle of the night. It was a breakthrough.

He dropped the prints on the table and yawned. The wall clock showed it was 2 A. M. and he thought about getting some sleep.

The phone rang. Wondering who it could be at this hour, he answered it.

"It's Matt, Piers. I had to call you."

"What's up?"

"Rufus hasn't come home. And Emma wasn't here when I got back."

"Could she be staying with somebody else?"

"She might be, but she usually tells me if she's going to do that. Thing is, Mandy's not here either."

"Mandy?"

"Her Companion. I've never known Emma to take her out overnight. I looked in Emma's room and it's a shambles. Stuff all over the place, drawers left open. And she's normally very tidy. I'm worried, Piers."

"Sit tight, I'm coming over." He hung up.

"I don't think so, Piers."

He hadn't heard Mr. T. come in.

"What was that?" Piers tried to sound casual, but that wasn't the way it came out.

"You heard." Mr. T.'s tone was harsh, his voice level. "We know you saw us tonight."

Piers felt a pang of fear. "Saw you?"

"It's no use pretending." Mr. T. was moving toward him. Under other circumstances, his rolling, almost comical gait would have amused Piers. Now it filled him with dread.

He searched desperately for something to say. "Look, T., I can see that some people have been unkind to Companions — "

The bear threw back his head and gave a short, hollow laugh.

" — and that perhaps I could have been more considerate. But if we work together, we can — "

"No, Piers. It's too late. What you know can harm us, and we've suffered too much to let you ruin things. I'm sorry." He extended his arm to the radio on the sideboard and snapped it on. Loud music boomed from it.

Then Piers saw the wickedly curved knife in Mr. T.'s other paw.

The sound of the radio smothered his screams.

The bear fed the last of the photographs into the fire in the hearth and tossed the negatives after them. He took the poker and jabbed at the burning mass. The dancing flames reflected in his glassy eyes and threw his enormous shadow on the walls and ceiling.

It was a pity about Piers, he thought. As humans went, he wasn't too bad. But it was a matter of survival now, and nobody could be allowed to stand in their way.

Still, he couldn't help remembering better times.

And a big round tear rolled down Mr. Thumpy's cheek.

THE HOUSE THAT JACK BUILT

Garry Kilworth

Caleb Jones was lost on Bodmin Moor with only a few litres of petrol in the tank of his car. It was twilight and the night was sweeping in like a soft cloud, purpling the bleak landscape. In the distance, perhaps a half kilometre away, stood a large foursquare house. A huge wooden structure with balconies and verandas, and gabled windows jutting from the roof, its timber planks gleamed red in the dying sun. Its lines were simple but its stature imposing. The house looked as if it had been dropped from the sky. There was no garden or yard, and the moor came right up to the walls.

Caleb stopped the car and cut the engine some hundred metres from the house.

The silence was awesome: no bird calls, no animal rustlings, not even the sound of the wind. He could see a copse of trees just behind

the house, on the far corner, but even this
was devoid of life or sound. A stream ran
through the spinney, curving in and out of the
moor.

He stared at the house, hoping to see signs
that it was lived in.

"It looks a bit spooky," he mutttered to
himself, then wished he hadn't spoken. The
sound of his own voice, in the midst of so much
silence, added to his feelings of unease.

Dark red shadows chased themselves over
the house as Caleb sat watching. It did indeed
look eerie. There were no lights at the windows and it appeared to be empty, yet it looked
in good repair. There was nothing neglected
about it. Perhaps it was a holiday home of some
kind? Though who would spend their vacation
out in the middle of nowhere?

There was nothing else for it: he had to see
if there was anyone at home. He started the
car again and drove up to the veranda, then
got out and went up the wooden steps to
the door. The timbers seemed to bend com-
fortably beneath his feet, giving him the impression that he was treading on something
soft.

"Strange," he murmured.

Again, the sound of his voice seemed to violate the silence.

He knocked on the door and waited, but received no answer, then he tried looking in at the window, but it was black inside. A sudden feeling of lethargy came over him. He was very, very tired. It was a warm night and there was no reason why he should not sleep on the porch. It looked very inviting, even though it was hard wood. He lay down, fully clothed. The boards beneath him were unusually comfortable and seemed to mould themselves to his shape.

Caleb awoke in the early morning, just as the dawn was creeping over the horizon. It felt a little chilly and damp on the veranda. He got up and found the front door handle. Turning it, he discovered the door was unlocked. He stood in the doorway and called, "Hey, anyone in?"

The stillness within seemed to be broken by a faint reply. Caleb felt embarassed. How would he explain himself at this time of the morning?

"Hello?" he called again. "Sorry to wake you. I — er — got lost . . ."

Again, that muffled reply. It sounded as if he was meant to enter the house. Caleb stepped inside. The front hallway smelled of beeswax and wood polish, but it was completely bare, not even a rug on the floor.

"Where shall I go?" he called, feeling foolish.

The front door suddenly slammed shut behind him with a soft thud. Caleb jumped and turned, startled by the sound. Plunged into near darkness, he began to panic for no reason. He rushed at the front door and tried to find the handle, but in the dimness couldn't locate it. Finally, with his heart racing, he stepped away from the door and surveyed it. There did not seem to *be* a handle. Had it dropped off when the door slammed shut?

"Hey!" he shouted, the panic still evident in his voice. "Where are you?"

In here.

"Where?"

Here.

The voice seemed to be coming from a room off the hallway. Caleb stepped into the room. He looked around him in the grey light coming from the glassless but barred window. He was stunned by what he saw. Beautiful dark oak panels decorated the walls, covered in wonderful carvings of cottages, houses, churches, buildings of all kinds. There was no ceiling, just red beams and a shiplap roof above. The beams too were carved, showing primitive villages with temples and longhouses. Were they Polynesian perhaps? Or Indonesian?

Staring through the window, Caleb could see the grey desolate moor beyond, stretching out flatly to a sharp horizon.

There was no one in the room and not a single stick of furniture. Not a curtain or rug. Nothing.

He turned to step back out into the hall when the room's heavy door slammed shut in his face.

"Hey!" he cried again, panic rising in him. "Hey, what's this . . . *Hey!*"

Again he could find no handle on the door. He began to hammer and kick at it, yelling for someone to let him out. He tried to hook his nails around the edge and prise the door open. The wood seemed to swell when he did this and jam the door tighter. He began to feel real fear now and rushed over to the window.

The wooden bars looked extremely strong. Caleb tried to wrench one of them free. It was hopeless. He kicked and punched the window bars, to try to loosen them. That was when he heard the voice again . . .

Leave the window alone.

"Wha . . . what?" he cried, swinging around, for the voice was very near now. The room was still empty.

Leave the window alone.

"Hey, you!" cried Caleb angrily. "Where are you? Let me out of here, damn you!"

Put your hand through the hole, said the rich baritone voice.

He looked around and saw a large knothole, as big as a fist, on an internal wall. There was nothing but darkness on the other side. What was this — a trick? Maybe there was a key or something on the other side of the hole. Or a lever to release the door. It was all too bizarre for him to think straight. He put his hand inside the hole and felt around. Nothing. But before he could withdraw his hand the knothole closed around his wrist. He was trapped like someone locked in old-fashioned village stocks.

He tried to wrench his hand free and only hurt his wrist.

"Ow! That's painful," he said.

Don't move then. Stay still. Just feel the wall vibrate. Can you feel it? That's my voice.

"Get lost!" shouted Caleb. "You crazy . . ."

The floor began to shake now, until Caleb was being rattled and jostled, up and down. The sound hurt his ears. His teeth clattered, his bones were jarred, his head shook. He was jolted off his feet and again his arm pained him as he pulled on it.

"Stop it, stop it!" he shrieked, as the whole room continued to shake violently.

It stopped a few moments later.

Now do as you're told.

"I'm going mad," whined Caleb. "I'm going crazy. If this is a trick, you should be ashamed. You're driving me insane."

The house rustled a sigh from somewhere up in the eaves.

Madness — the human answer to anything unusual. Very well, consider yourself insane if you wish. It matters little to me, so long as you remain here.

"Who . . . who are you?"

Caleb was told that it was the house itself who was speaking to him. It told him he was now a prisoner and would remain so until he died. The house explained that it was immobile and could not care for itself.

Therefore I need another creature, a human such as yourself, to do the work for me. I need someone to wax me inside and out as protection against the weather. I need repairs and maintenance. I need you.

"I can't do that," cried Caleb. "You can't keep me here like this. What am I doing, talking to a house? This is sheer lunacy. Look, I can't stay here. You're talking about slavery — a slave. I can't stay here."

You will stay here — you have no choice.

Caleb tried to calm down and think. He could do nothing while the wall had his hand trapped. If he was to do any maintenance, he would need to move around the building. Once the knothole let him go, and the door opened, he could run.

"All right," he said. "I'll do it. Let me go. Show me where the tools are . . ."

The knothole widened and allowed Caleb to withdraw his hand. He rubbed his sore wrist. Then he walked slowly towards the door. The door opened. Caleb stepped into the hall, his heart pattering quickly. He stood under the wide curving staircase, which rose in a majestic sweep to the next floor, and considered what he should say next.

"Can I just get some tools from the boot of my car?" he asked the house.

There was stillness for a few moments, then the front door swung open.

Caleb stepped through the front door and down to the car. Then he quickly opened the door and jumped into the driver's seat, fumbling with his keys. From outside there came the sound of wood under tension: a straining of timbers that screamed for release. Caleb started the car. Triumphantly he put it in gear and began to pull away. He glanced at the house and saw that one corner of the veranda was squeezing itself, putting the timbers under enormous pressure.

Suddenly, one of the veranda posts gave way with a crack like a rifle shot and went flashing through the air. It struck the front of the car like a javelin, smashing through the engine, entering the inside of the cab through the dashboard in a ripping and tearing of wires, plastic and metal. The jagged end of the spar stopped just half a centimetre away from Caleb's chest, right over the spot where his heart was beating.

Caleb screamed, terrified, knowing that he had almost been impaled on the veranda post. He wriggled out from behind the wheel, scratching his chest on the broken spar. Then he fell through the open door onto the ground.

The car had stopped, the engine completely wrecked. Oil glugged on the ground. There was a smell of petrol in the air. Caleb lay there, sobbing. He knew he could not run. The house would kill him before he got ten metres away. If it could hurl corner posts like javelins, it could send out a dart-sized splinter, or a spray of slivers like grapeshot, and cut him down like a running hare.

Caleb looked up at the sky. It was a heavy day with thick clouds, matching his own feelings. He was no longer free. He was a prisoner.

Your first job, said the house, *will be to repair the veranda. You will find seasoned wood stacked in the lean-to shed on the south side. You will also prepare more lumber for future use. The copse behind me is the source of my materials. Cut down only the mature trees, and do it with sympathy and understanding. Do not touch the fruit bushes and trees, for you will need their produce later.*

"What if I don't?"
Then you will surely die.

The house was not completely satisfied with Caleb's repairs, even though he was a reasonable carpenter.

You will have to learn better, it warned him.

He worked long hours, with little satisfaction, but gradually, despite himself, he could not help admiring his own workmanship as it improved. The house itself had been built to exacting standards, fashioned by expert hands. The rooms on the first story were clad in carved panels too, decorated this time with curlicues in their corners and centres, and there were natural shapes too — a sheaf of corn on one, an oak leaf on another.

Most of the rooms were plain, it was true, but there was something about the feel of wood which gratified Caleb. He found he was touching the house, constantly running his hand over a rail or pillar. Nothing was painted, the bare wood having been polished overall with beeswax.

The house moved all the time. Mostly it was just a gentle vibration, but ocasionally it creaked and swayed like a whale, reminding

Caleb that it was a beast and not an inanimate object. Sometimes it felt inclined to talk and did so in those same deep tones that he had heard on first entering its door, its oak panels vibrating as it did so. These were its vocal cords, each room a mouth.

Four of the house's eight bedrooms were stocked high with provisions for the human occupant. No doubt the original builder of the house had been responsible for this. There were enough canned goods to last for many years. Part of the copse was an orchard which grew apples, pears and plums. There were also gooseberry and blackcurrant bushes. A vegetable patch, which he was expected to tend, provided Caleb with potatoes, cabbages and other fresh fare, and the stream provided him with water. The house would not allow him to starve, though it never permitted him to overeat either.

The house never slept. It kept constant watch on its prisoner.

There were many cupboards in the house, but there was one whose door would never open. Caleb was struggling with this door one day, when the house asked him what he was doing.

"I want to look inside," said Caleb.

Why?

"Because . . . because it's the only cupboard that seems locked. I'm curious."

All right.

The cupboard door swung open and when Caleb saw what was inside he gasped and reeled backwards, clutching his throat in horror. Inside the narrow cupboard was the remains of a human being — a skeleton in rags — held up by wooden pegs. The eyeless sockets of a former tenant stared bleakly out from its final resting place in the house. Caleb slammed the door of the cupboard shut and screamed at the house.

"What was that? Tell me!"

The house told him this was the last slave it had owned, after its builder had left. The man had been a hiker, crossing the moor, and had fallen into the house's clutches.

He died too soon. I gave him a grave in one of my many pockets.

"You mean you *worked* him to death!"

Too soon.

"Too soon for what?"

But the house declined to answer.

"It's horrible . . ." shrieked Caleb.

It's just a dead man, nothing more, said the house.

Caleb saw in that cupboard what his eventual fate was to be.

The next time he was out tending the vegetable patch, he dropped his rake and ran. He had barely made two metres before he was brought down by a long white root, dripping soil, which reared like a snake out of the earth and whipped itself around his ankle. He was dragged back and ordered into the house, and was punished by being locked in a room for two days without food or water. The house was a harsh taskmaster and would stand no resistance.

You will do as you are told, it ordered.

Caleb came out of the room after two days, and went straight to his larder, but on the way a narrow cupboard door swung open. He peered warily inside, but it was empty.

"What did you do that for?" he asked the house.

I wanted to show you, replied the house.

"But there's nothing in there."

Not yet. It's for you — if you die too soon.

Caleb took the warning.

*   *   *

One evening, while he was sitting on the veranda, Caleb asked the house about its foundations. The house told him that it had roots, like a tree, which held it fast to the earth. It was one of these that had lassoed Caleb the day he had tried to run away.

Caleb suppressed a shudder. There was a picture in his mind of the thing that held him prisoner; a giant octopus-like creature with grey tentacles that reached down into the dirt. The trees were part of the house too, growing from its roots. It could produce its own parts but needed a human to fashion them into shape: to shave them, smooth them with sandpaper, and finally wax them to a polished finish. The house welcomed no other visitors. No birds settled in its eaves, no mice lived behind the wainscotting. No ant or cockroach settled in a crack that was not instantly crushed.

Nor would it have furniture touching its glossy floors.

Caleb reluctantly agreed with the house that he too received some benefit from the situation. He was very fit and well. The physical exercise was good for him. He had no real ties in the outside world. His parents had been killed in a car accident and his girlfriend had left him, so there was no one to miss him. He had been on his way to the Cornish coast, to work on a caravan site, when the house had ensnared him.

"Who made you?" Caleb asked the house.

Something.

"Who was he? What was his name?"

He doesn't have a name.

"Was he — is it a human being?" asked Caleb.

It's almost human.

A chill went through Caleb. Something occurred to him, and he said "Is this house a trap — like a mouse trap? Does it catch things for the — the almost-human?"

The house did not answer this question and Caleb could get no more out of it about the possible owner, if indeed there was one. So he changed the subject. He knew better than to try to trick the house into revealing weaknesses, so he always asked direct questions. The house often gave simple, straightforward answers, as on this occasion.

"Are you afraid of anything?" asked Caleb.

Fire, said the house without hesitation. *I fear the threat of fire.*

This might have been useful to Caleb, had he any way of making fire, but he had not.

"I think," said Caleb, trying to lighten the conversation, "the person who built this house was called *Jack*. I think this is 'The House That Jack Built.' "

The house asked him what he meant and Caleb told it the story of "The House That Jack Built." The house loved the tale and asked for more stories about houses, and Caleb recounted "The Three Little Pigs," "Hansel and Gretel," *The Little House on the Prairie,* and one or two others. When he had run out of stories, he began to think about how much humans came to regard houses as live things. They cared for them like pets and in some cases almost worshipped them.

I like the stories, said the house, and thereafter it was more lenient with Caleb.

Two years came and went and Caleb toiled, ever watching for a chance to escape. In the winter it was deadly cold, though the house could summon a certain warmth from its walls by vibrating them. Caleb survived, but barely. It was a miserable existence.

There were certain things he liked about the house. On the days when he inspected it for maintenance problems he found himself running his hands over the smooth wooden banisters as his eyes took in the solid timber hallway where the grain in the walls flowed gloriously in brown rivers to the archways of the ceiling. Knots and whorls in the wood formed eddies and currents. There were firm stanchions, straight as ship masts, and beautiful curving buttresses supporting some of the inner walls.

The whole house had been fashioned to perfection by a craftsman. Its doors and frames were flush with one another, with wooden hinges held by wooden pegs, lubricated with vegetable oil. There was a rustic splendour to the hewn beams that shouldered the roof. There was a balance of all its parts.

These were the aspects of the house that Caleb liked.

His main grievance was that he remained a prisoner of the house, to do its bidding.

Finally he hit upon a plan of escape.

Bit by bit, over a period of time, he managed to divert the stream that ran through the copse. Every time he went to pick fruit, or tend the vegetable patch, he secretly dropped a stone into the stream. Gradually, as the water began to find a new course away from the house, the house became more and more lethargic in its responses. It needed a great deal of liquid to sustain it and that water was drying up.

What's happening? said the house. *I don't understand why I'm feeling so tired.*

Caleb was clever enough not to lie.

"I don't think you're getting enough water," he replied. "There's only a trickle in the brook these days. It must be something to do with the weather."

Fetch me more water.

"I can't bring you what isn't there," said Caleb. "You'll have to make sure you get enough when it rains."

The house complained about this, but it rained that night and little more was said.

A month later, there was a long period of drought, when no rain fell. Caleb said to the house, "Shall I see if there's something blocking the stream, out on the moor?"

The house mumbled wearily that something
had to be done.

With his heart beating fast, Caleb took a
spade and walked out onto the moor, following
the old dry course of the stream. With each
step he got further and further away from his
master, beyond the reach of the roots. Finally
the house called, *That's far enough — don't go
any further*.

At that moment Caleb dropped the spade
and ran. A few moments later a huge chunk
of wood whistled by his ear and buried itself
in the turf just ahead of him.

Come back or I'll kill you! thundered the
house.

Caleb's work had made him very fit and
strong, however, and he increased his speed.
Normally, the house would have been accurate
with its missiles, but it was exhausted by lack
of water and severely out of sorts, and its aim
was not as good as it should have been.

More slivers of wood hurtled past Caleb,
zipping into the heather. He kept on running,
ignoring the threats from the house, praying
that he would not be hit. Eventually he was
out of range of the flying weapons, and stopped
to get his breath. He turned and shook his fist

triumphantly in the direction of the house, shouting, "I beat you at last! I hope you dry up and rot. You'll never see me again, that's for sure!"

With that he walked until he found the nearest road and then made his way to a town.

Caleb sincerely thought he would never return to the house, until one evening he got into an argument with someone in a pub. He had been telling a crowd about his experience with the house and one man had challenged him, calling him a liar.

"Right," said Caleb, a little drunk. "I swore I would never go back to the house again, but if one or two of you come with me, I'm willing to go. We'll have to take weapons with us, otherwise the house will try to kill us."

"What sort of weapons?" sneered the man who had called him a liar.

"Petrol," said Caleb grimly. "And matches."

So the small group got in a car and drove out onto Bodmin Moor, the driver following Caleb's directions. Now that he was actually returning, Caleb felt some apprehension. The effect of the drink was wearing off and his old fears began to return. The house was a very powerful creature. Even the threat of fire might not be enough to control it. He began to get scared, even though he had others with him. The house was not going to be very pleasant to him if it managed to get him back into its clutches. He could not let that happen.

He ordered the driver to stop the car several hundred metres away from the house, which was not clearly visible on the moonlit moor.

"You go and see it," said Caleb. "I'll wait here."

"What are you scared of?" scoffed one of the men. "There's nothing there but a few planks of wood."

"Go and see," repeated Caleb.

So the men got out of the car, laughing and joking, and went across the moor to enter the house. Caleb watched them go in, keeping the motor running in case he had to make a quick getaway. Eventually, much to his surprise, the group came out again, still jeering and scoffing. They strolled back to the car.

"Nothing but an empty old shack," said one of them. "You had us going there for a bit — I almost believed you . . ."

"I didn't," said the man who had called Caleb

a liar. "I knew all along he was pulling our legs."

Caleb got out of the car and walked slowly toward the house, mystified by what the men had told him. As he got closer, he could see it looked empty and hollow. It seemed like a husk, a fibrous thing with no life in it: the chaff without the wheat. It was dry, lacking in suppleness and strength.

"It's dead," he said to himself. "The house has died — through the lack of water, I expect."

At that moment the car roared off, the other men shouting and yelling insults, leaving Caleb behind.

His instinct was to run after them, try to get them to stop, but they were gone before he had covered ten metres.

"Damn people!" he said, angrily.

He turned back towards the house and studied it further. It struck him, not for the first time, that the house might be worth a lot of money. He knew it did not belong to anyone — no one living, that is — and he could claim it as his own. He could dispose of it as he wished and no one would stop him. Now that it was just dead wood, its supernatural life having drained away since it had been starved of sustenance, it could be sold on the open market.

"The cash for a house like that," Caleb murmured, "could set me up for a good few years to come."

He walked slowly up to the front door, where the men had gone in and out, and saw that it hung from one hinge. There was a certain amount of disrepair which needed to be put right before he could put the house on the market.

He stepped onto the wooden stairs that led up to the veranda. They no longer felt soft underfoot, like a thick carpet, but solid and firm. They were reassuringly dead timber. He walked the length of the porch, inspecting this and that, making sure there was no dry or wet rot setting in. Then finally he entered the house by the front door.

He stood for a while in the hallway, looking about him in the moonlight, remembering the first time he had entered the house. The red wood gleamed in the beams from the moon, entering through the barred windows and open door. Shadows of clouds drifted through the house. All was as still and as peaceful as death.

Then, suddenly, the silence was broken by a faint, single creak.

Caleb's heart jumped, but he told himself that all houses made noises, even dead ones.

As he stood there, he glanced through the open door of one of the rooms. Through the window of that room, out on the moor, he could see something glistening, silver in the moon's brightness. He stared hard at this snaking ribbon of light, suddenly realizing what it was he was looking at. The stream — it was the stream! Someone had unblocked it and it was once again on its old course. Did that mean the house was now able to drink again? Would it revive itself now there was water? And who had taken away his dam?

Caleb turned quickly and peered through the open doorway at the dirt road beyond. His instincts told him to run, *run quickly*, get away from that place, *run, run, run*.

There was a shuffling sound in the shadows at the back of the hall. Caleb stifled a scream as the fear rose in his throat. He wanted to run but now his legs wouldn't move.

So, you've come back? something said.

The voice was not that of the house. It was not a deep tone, of vibrating oak panels, but

one of a much higher and disconcerting pitch.
Caleb stared hard. There *was* something
there, the colour of an old root — it was something not very tall, not very smooth, something . . . not very human. It spoke again in
shrill, accusing tones.

What have you done to my house?

Caleb ran.

THE
STATION
WITH NO
NAME

Colin Greenland

THE STATION IS THERE. YOU DON'T ALWAYS pass it — only sometimes, going under the river. The trains that do go that way don't stop there. Nothing stops there any more. It's the station with no name.

It's probably only an ordinary station, one they closed down for some reason a long time ago. Perhaps the roof fell in and hurt somebody. Perhaps people were buried under the rubble for some time, and afterwards no one could bear to use it, so they locked it up and left it.

There's hardly enough light to see by, only a sort of mucky, grudging, dark brown light that filters down from somewhere up above. It looks like the bottom of the sea. You can just about make out the platforms, the exits like low square mouths full of darkness.

As your train passes through, though, the

same thing happens almost every time. You go over some kind of fault or bump in the track, and the train wheels spark, and at that instant that whole place lights up, stark and lifeless in the cold white glare. You see the bare walls, the locked gates, the shrouds of dust over everything like an abandoned tomb. It's only for an instant. If you happen to be looking down at that moment you'd never know it was there, the station with no name.

Mark and Kix hadn't even meant to go that way that night. They had been mucking about up the District Line when this bloke came after them and they had to run. They'd had to jump two trains to lose him, and that had taken them right out of ZEE-5's territory.

Mark wasn't happy about that. For one thing, he hadn't finished his throw, and that always got him annoyed. For another, he didn't know whose territory this was, exactly.

Kix was laughing his face off though, as always. Kix always had a good time, whatever. He looked around the car, picking out names they knew.

"STAC, look! POET! FA-Z!

Mark didn't care whose name there was. There was only one name he cared about.

Kix was mad, a crazy man — he didn't care about anything. It didn't bother him that they'd had to fall through the doors of a train that was going the wrong way. Mark took things like that personally. He didn't want to be heading south of the river. He had no business down that way. Anyway, it was nowhere. Who ever went down there? No one.

Kix was complaining happily. "I was really going good there," he was saying. "I was just getting the highlights, *fsss* . . ." He imitated himself spraying the ceiling of the train, next to POET and someone's orange blur that had dripped and run.

Mark wasn't listening. He had been staring out of the window and had seen a flare of electricity light up the station with no name.

He had seen the walls of brown tiles with little veins in them like marble, and the big blank medallions where the station name should be, and the platforms with black spiky railings blocking all the exits. It was dark again now, the shadows pulled in tight, but the light had flashed and shown him the station.

The train hadn't stopped. There wasn't supposed to be a station there. There was no station on the map.

None of that bothered Mark. What made *him* light up — what made tonight a good night suddenly, a really spectacular night, in fact — was that there was a station, and nobody had hit it yet! It was incredible. When the train light had splashed the walls, there was no answering dazzle of paint. No BAF, no DIET, not even 230 — and 230 was everywhere.

Kix, naturally, had missed it. "You're such a nerd, Kix," said Mark.

Kix pulled out his can. He aimed it at Mark and pretended to spray him. He grinned. Mark didn't grin back. Miles too late, Kix looked out of the window, as if sensing something had happened. He saw nothing. There was nothing to see.

They got off at the next stop, jumped the barrier and ran along the road and round a corner into a smelly bit of wasteland behind a supermarket. On the back wall of the shop they bombed a couple of locals — ESKIMO and DODGE, total unknowns — then Kix said he had to go home.

"My dad's coming," he said.

"Your dad?" Mark said. "He won't come." Kix gave a massive grin. "No," he said.

Mark, who had two parents, which was two

too many, couldn't let it go at that. He felt like leaning on Kix, pushing him with it. "Your dad never comes," Mark said.

Kix laughed, but it was weak, not a real Kix cackle. His dad was the only thing Kix didn't think was just one huge joke. "No, but," he said. "I just got to go, right?"

"Yer!" jeered Mark. "Go on, then."

As if he had been waiting for permission, Kix put his can in his pocket, pulled his cap straight, pulled his jacket straight. He laughed a sneering, happy laugh and departed.

Mark sprayed a hard burst of blue at the wet black rubbish lying around. He was glad Kix had gone. Now he could really move. He gave Kix five minutes, then went back to the station, keeping out of sight of the man at the barrier. There was a local map on the wall by the entrance. Mark studied it, memorizing street names. Then he ran out, and off in another direction.

He ran along a street of factories with shuttered doors. VACANCIES said the boards, in white letters, but all the card slots underneath were empty. Perhaps those were the vacancies they meant.

Mark's footsteps on the pavement were

quiet, as though the street wanted to hide his presence. No one else was about, and there was hardly any traffic. He went left and cut across a yard. He was following the train line.

He ran across a road and behind a line of hoardings with posters for rum and Rothman's and car tyres. The street lights showed that kids had been at the posters, but Mark didn't pay any attention to that. Only dweebs bombed posters.

He scrambled behind the hoardings, out of the light, and found a dusty brick building. It was two small shops, gutted and boarded up, with a dark gap in between.

That was it. It had to be.

In the gap was a door. It wasn't the proper door — it was a door from somewhere else that they'd brought and nailed into place. There had been glass in the door once. Now there was plywood blocking the hole where the glass had been. Some of the plywood was just hanging there, loose. It had been ripped away in one go, as though someone big had come this way in a temper.

Mark squeezed through the hole in the door.

Inside it was utterly black. One foot at a time, Mark crept across the floor away from the door. The floor felt like tile — big tiles and grit and rubbish lying around.

He got out his lighter, shook it, turned the flame up full and flicked it on.

He was in a circular hall with empty ticket windows and ancient yellow tube maps, so strange you could hardly tell what they were. There were triangular sooty marks at the top of the walls as though they used to light the place with candles. Turning to look behind him he glimpsed a pair of sentry boxes for ticket collectors and a big hole going down into the ground. Then the lighter got hot and he had to let it go out.

Mark stood there in the dark, breathing the musty, shut-up air. This place was just incredible! He felt like an explorer breaking into a pyramid in Egypt. There was no gold, unless you counted the dull brass trim around the glass of the ticket windows; no priceless old pots, only empty bottles of cider and battered beer cans. What there was was something better. Bare space. Yards and yards and yards of it. And not a fleck of paint anywhere.

Mark flicked his lighter again and laughed. He was pleased with himself. He was glad he hadn't told Kix about this. He imagined Kix's face when he brought him down this way next. He would wait until it was just coming up, then he'd hold his hand up mysteriously and point out of the train window. And Kix would look, and at that second the lightning would flash out from under the wheels, and there it would be — the whole place one gigantic throw, both sides of the track, all his!

First, he had to get down on the platform. And he had to do it now, this minute, while his head was full of it and his blood was up. The Name would not hang about.

Putting his lighter away to save it, Mark moved carefully forwards. He could make out the shape of the two boxes, and behind them a big black hole in the soft, grey, clinging dark.

He stood on the brink of the hole, blinking in the tiny breeze that blew cold air and grit from far below. His eyes grew used to the gloom. He could see what was beneath him now: two deep pits, shockingly huge, where the escalators had been torn out; and over to one side, a half-open door.

Mark went to the door and pushed through it. There was a black iron spiral staircase, leading straight down into the ground.

Going down in total blackness, he flicked his

lighter only once. Nothing showed through the gratings beneath his feet. His trainers, so quiet on the street, sounded loud and clumsy on the metal stairs. In the shaft there was no breeze. The air was dead. Thick cobwebs trailed in his face.

Mark emerged at the bottom. He could see weak light leaking through from the platform. It showed him high railings barring his way. He fumbled about and found a gate without a handle. He shook it. It was locked. The railings were rigid, the cross-bars too far apart to climb. Mark jammed his foot against one of the uprights and tried to bend it, but it wouldn't give.

He kicked the railings. There was a dull metal thud; and after it a small, dry pattering sound that whispered away through the dark like shuffling feet. Mark held his breath, listening. The noise did not come again. It was probably just the rattle of a train, far away in the tunnels.

He stumbled around the lower hall until he found the bottom of the escalator bank. Underneath he could just make out a lot of metal brackets and supports. Climbing a little way into the dark hole, he planted his feet firmly and got hold of a strut — a long strip of steel with round holes in it. Putting all his weight on it, he bent it away from where it was bolted. Then he jiggled it until he could swing it around on its bolt and hauled it back, bending it the other way.

For several minutes Mark worked on the strut, loosening it. He worked on it so hard he didn't notice the eyes gathering around him in the darkness until there were quite a lot of them.

He felt the hairs on his arms bristle. He whipped out his lighter and flicked it on.

Rats. Black rats, big ones black as coal, creeping up out of the depths of the escalator pit to watch him. They didn't seem to mind his flame and didn't even move until he stamped his foot. Then they turned tail and vanished, instantly.

Mark breathed hard. He put away his lighter. He heaved on his strut.

The eyes were back.

With a shout, he snapped the strut off. It was good and heavy. He swung it round his head like a rat-killing club. He felt good. "I am the Name!" he told the rats.

He bashed the side of the pit with his strut

and then climbed out and went back to the iron railing where the gate was. He hit the gate three times, aiming right at the lock. On the third try the lock gave with a sweet, smart crack and the gate swung open as though he was only too welcome to come through to the platform; as though it had been waiting all this time for him and him alone.

The station with no name lay like a sunken wreck at the bottom of the dark brown sea. Beyond the crevasse of the rails, the other platform leaned away in the murk, curving like the hull of a big ship. There were the blank signs, the blocked exits, the empty spaces where posters were supposed to go; the long window of the waiting room like an unmarked slab of slate. All ready and waiting for him.

Mark threw his strut into a corner with a resounding clang and stood square to the wall. He listened to the big hollow silence of the underground, the tunnels running off for miles to every corner of the city. He made an announcement, in the Caribbean voice he liked to use sometimes when he was alone. "I mek my Mark," he said. He shook his can. The ball bearing rattled crisply inside — the sound of eagerness. Mark started to write.

He put his initials on each of the doorposts. Just warming up. Winding up to it, like a footballer before the match: Mark v. the Rest of the World. No contest, really. He sprinted down the platform, ready to open up some of this *space*.

Okay. O.K. The Name. A large specimen. Something to make the Monday morning cattle blink in disapproval as the lightning flared and it leapt out at them. Here, right in the big station sign. In all the station signs, each end of the platform and in the middle. Starting here.

Mark made an M. The M he made did not look like an M. If it looked like anything, it looked like a fat blue balloon with invisible rubber bands wrapped round it. It gleamed down at him from the tiles. It was very blue, like a streak of sky glimpsed through the roof of a cave.

Mark whooped. His voice rang in the lifeless halls of the station with no name.

He shifted his stance, stood with his feet wide apart; shook up again; did the A. The A was like a razor unfolding, hooked in the fat side of the M. The wide curves of the M and the wicked thin curves of the A looked good together like that. Mark did the R, propped against them. The flick up at the end of the R was neat and sweet.

"Sweet as de banana on de tree," said Mark, aloud.

As soon as he stopped speaking, he heard the small whispering sound again. This time it sounded like someone in one of the passages crumpling up some paper. It was such a tiny sound, you would think you could hardly hear it, but in the deep silence of the station with no name Mark could hear it very clearly.

He knew now it was just the rats, or else dirt sifting down from the old brickwork, disturbed by his own movements most probably. Nothing had moved down here for years by the looks of it. But the tiny noise gave Mark a sudden overwhelming sense of being completely alone, in the dark, far underground, in a place no one even knew was there. No one would come here to look for him. Not even the rest of ZEE-5.

Mark worked a lot on his own, of course. But most of the time the others were not far off. Even if there was no one else, Kix would usually be hanging around. For a minute, Mark almost wished someone else was here, not

Kix, but Poet or Norman or someone, to admire his handwriting and keep guard. ZEE-5 — it was a really slick logo. Should he do that somewhere?

No chance, he thought. Let them find their own deserted station. Later, when they see what I've done, the others will be all over it. A major ZEE-5 raid! He smiled. He did the first bit of the K, with the fins that always made him think of combs, and then a slashing upstroke.

"What do you think you're doing?"

The hoarse voice was close. The shock of it was like needles in his ear. His spine contracted painfully.

He spun round and saw an old man standing there. An old man with long white hair and a white beard — white, but also yellow and brown and matted with filth. He was wearing a ragged coat and trousers that unravelled halfway down his calves, and boots tied up with string.

A wino! A wino had nearly made him muck up his throw!

Mark scowled. "Interior decorating," he said.

"Young vandal. Should be horse-whipped."

The voice was like an old door creaking in the wind. The man shuffled close, trailing shreds of newspaper after him, carrying something awkwardly under his arm. He was as thin as a rail and his eyes were sunk so deep in his skull you couldn't see them at all. He was obviously in a world of his own.

Mark turned away from the stink. "Where did you come from?" he asked.

"Up the street," said the old man impatiently. A sheet of newspaper under his foot lifted in the breeze from the tunnel, tearing slowly as it fluttered.

"I haven't got any change," Mark lied, lifting his can.

"I don't want your money," said the old man contemptuously.

Mark sighed. He lowered his can again. This old bloke had put him right off. He could barely see where he had been going to go with the rest of the K.

He turned to the man. "Look, just get out of here, all right? Just go away." He tried to push him away without touching him. People like that shouldn't be walking around on their own. He barely looked human. And he smelled something terrible. "Go on. Right away."

"Young thug! I shall report you . . ." The old man lurched back along the platform, clutching his luggage to his withered chest. Mark could see the remains of a briefcase, tied up badly with a lot of cord and string. The two halves of it were slipping apart, scattering more ragged paper in the dust. As he wrestled with it, the old man looked to Mark like an ancient commuter, lost on his way home. He hadn't had the brains not to take a train he didn't know, and so he'd been stuck here, forever.

"How *did* you get in, anyway?" asked Mark. "You didn't jump off a train."

"No trains until they clear the line!" nagged the man, plucking at one of the tattered papers protruding from his case, as if it was a document to prove the point. "The bombers got the line." He said it as if Mark was supposed to know what he was talking about.

He was getting on Mark's nerves. "The bombers got your brain more like," he said. "The line's not blocked. I came that way, right?" he said, pointing with his thumb. "And the train went that way. So." He felt better now, more in command. "You're not supposed to be here any more than I am, so just belt up, all right?"

The old man came skating towards him, faster than a wreck like him had any business to. There was black mould on his clothes, and big dark blotches on his skin. He opened his horrible mouth wide, practically in Mark's face. He had a grin bigger than Kix's.

Mark shook up hard and started spraying again.

"Pack you off up the front and let Hitler sort you out!" wheezed the old man contemptuously.

"Get lost, granddad! I'm warning you."

Where now? Mark strode away from his prosecutor, along the platform. There, the timetable! Shrivelled paper pasted on the wall — no one wanted to read that any more. MARK MARK MARK. He was in his stride now, whipping each one off in three moves, five seconds, less.

Then someone else turned up. Another one of them! A woman, this one was — a young woman thin and white as a fish, in a headscarf and carpet slippers that were rotting on her feet. She came tottering out of nowhere with her hands stretched out. "Mister," she whispered. "Please mister, have you seen my Betty?"

She put her hand on Mark's arm. It was cold and damp as a lump of putty. A wet, bad smell came off her. Not alcohol. Not even meths or glue. Her voice was soft and weak as a moth scrambling inside a lampshade. "Please mister, have you seen my Betty?"

At that moment there was a noise in the south-bound tunnel. A light. A train coming.

Without thinking, Mark seized hold of her cold hand and pulled her back in the shadow of a pillar. The train, a track maintenance rig, clanked slowly past, long and blind and low and yellow. The woman stood behind Mark until the train had gone. She was so close her smell enveloped him, making him feel sick. She was worse than the old man.

Here came the old man now, shambling towards them. He was getting so animated, bits were falling off him. "Is this young layabout interfering with you, madam?" he creaked. "Fetch the station master!"

Mark pushed him away, hard. It was like pushing a greasy sack full of chickenbones and jelly. "You stupid old dosser! You just stay out of my way, right?"

"But my Betty," whined the woman, helplessly. "She's not even four . . ."

"She's not down here," said Mark. "Go and look somewhere else."

He could see now that the woman was not as young as she had first seemed. Her mouth was a mass of wrinkles. She seemed very ill. Her eyes, like the old man's, were black holes in her chalky face. Below, shiny wet lines trailed down either cheek, as though a snail had crawled up into each socket.

"There were so many people . . . and she's so little . . ."

Mark wrenched away from her. What did they have to bother him for? What difference did it make to a couple of derelicts if he had the station? It wasn't their station anyway. It was his.

"Mister . . ."

Mark set his teeth and worked on.

In a while Number Three turned up. This one was wearing a London Underground uniform, or the rags of one, decaying and caked with filth. His grey hair sprouted up through the crown of his cap like a frost-bitten bush.

"Oh my God!" said Mark wearily. He felt his stomach heave as the man approached. Grimly he concentrated on the angle of an A.

"You're not supposed to be on my station," said the man, in a voice like a frog shut in a filing cabinet.

"You want to look after it better, if it's yours," said Mark loudly.

"You shouldn't be down here," the man persisted. "You ought to be in the main shelter."

"You ought to be locked up," said Mark.

"What's your name?" the man demanded.

"Donald Duck," said Mark. MARK, he squirted.

"I haven't got you on my list," said the man, and then he gave a low chuckle.

Mark had had enough. He was obviously completely loopy, like his mates. "Go and play with your trains!" said Mark, starting to move towards the stairs.

"You won't get any trains here, sonny," called the "station master" with pride. "The trains don't stop here any more."

Something in that gloating croak made Mark pause. He looked back uncertainly at the decrepit silhouette. "You've been down here too long," he said.

"Since the warning . . ." the figure cried, and the echoes rang and ebbed away to nothing along the tunnel.

Mark was running up the stairs. At the top he looked back. The old fraud was stumbling after him, lurching slowly towards the staircase. Mark laughed. He couldn't catch him in a million years. He probably couldn't even get upstairs.

Mark ran across the bridge, lazily, arms and legs flying free. He felt as if he could leap down to the platform in one enormous jump. He did it in three.

He looked back across the rails. They were all there, both men and the old woman too, lined up at the edge of the platform, watching him. The first old man was still holding his distintegrating briefcase, clutching it to him as though he thought someone was going to take it away from him. The woman was clasping his arm, stroking distractedly at wisps of ancient hair escaping from her scarf like stuffing from a ruined armchair. The man who thought he was the station master was standing in a strange posture, leaning forward, running his hands slowly up and down his front. There was a kind of eagerness about them, like an audience assembled for a pop concert. Mark saw a glimmer of drool fall from the station master's mouth and drop onto the tracks. They couldn't take their eyes off him.

It was just like being on stage. Mark was the star. He would give them a performance, all right!

He capered for them, swivelling his hips. He strutted up the platform, taunting them. "You can't fool me. The war was fifty years ago. You couldn't have been here all that time. You wouldn't still be alive!"

He shouted louder. His voice rang across the lightless gulf. "You're nuts, all of you. You don't even know what year it is. Why don't you go and bother the Salvation Army? Go and set fire to yourself under the bridge with the rest of your mates! Yer, go on!"

Tiring of them, he went to see if he could get in the waiting room. He could do a little redecorating in there. He put his hand on the doorknob and, stiffly, it turned. Mark went inside.

Went into the waiting room, where the others were. All of them. Quite a lot of them altogether, waiting in the waiting room at the station with no name, huddled over their belongings, their grimy shopping bags filled with slats of broken crates and butchers' knives. In every corner they sat and stood and perched, among heaps of slimy bones and hanks of hair and empty shoes. Their faces were veiled with the cobwebs the spiders had spun across them and rats had eaten their feet, but still they stood up when Mark entered the room — stood up to welcome him.

It was only right and proper. Mark was the Name.

Kix thought it was all right, riding in the back of the police car. He leaned across the copper to look out the window, to see if he could spot anyone he knew on the street. The copper pushed him back in his seat.

The driver was on the radio, talking in codes and numbers. It was just like on the telly. "Why can't we have the siren going?" said Kix, goofily.

"Leave it out," the copper grunted.

"Round here you last saw him, was it?" called the driver.

Kix pointed through the windscreen. "Down behind the TruSave," he said.

They spent a long while poking around the back of the supermarket, rattling doors and stirring the rubbish in the bins with a long bit of wood.

Finally they told Kix to go home. "Buy a ticket," the copper advised him, looking him straight in the eye. Kix sniggered.

On the platform he saw a POET and a lot of fresh JAWJs. He wished he'd brought his can, but the cops would only have taken it off him. Then the train came in and he got on it, and sat looking at his reflection in the black window.

That was how he came to see Mark's great throw. There was a big white electric flash suddenly, and there it was. Kix yelped aloud and knelt on the seats, pressing his face to the window. It was brilliant! It was everywhere, all over the place! MARK, MARK, MARK everywhere in huge great sprays. It was great. It was the greatest! As the train rocked on and the after-image faded Kix laughed and laughed, while the other people in the carriage frowned and tried to look as if he wasn't there.

He wondered why Mark had changed his colour. He had been using blue but there was no sign of any blue back there. It was all red: bright red and sticky-looking, as if it was still wet.

THRILLERS

Nobody Scares 'Em Like

R.L. Stine

THRILLERS

D.E. Athkins
- ☐ MC45246-0 Mirror, Mirror — $3.25
- ☐ MC45349-1 The Ripper — $3.25

A. Bates
- ☐ MC45829-9 The Dead Game — $3.25
- ☐ MC43291-5 Final Exam — $3.25
- ☐ MC44582-0 Mother's Helper — $3.25
- ☐ MC44238-4 Party Line — $3.25

Caroline B. Cooney
- ☐ MC44316-X The Cheerleader — $3.25
- ☐ MC41641-3 The Fire — $3.25
- ☐ MC43806-9 The Fog — $3.25
- ☐ MC45681-4 Freeze Tag — $3.25
- ☐ MC45402-1 The Perfume — $3.25
- ☐ MC44884-6 The Return of the Vampire — $2.95
- ☐ MC41640-5 The Snow — $3.99
- ☐ MC45680-6 The Stranger — $3.50
- ☐ MC45682-2 The Vampire's Promise — $3.50

Richie Tankersley Cusick
- ☐ MC43115-3 April Fools — $3.25
- ☐ MC43203-6 The Lifeguard — $3.25
- ☐ MC43114-5 Teacher's Pet — $3.25
- ☐ MC44235-X Trick or Treat — $3.50

Carol Ellis
- ☐ MC46411-6 Camp Fear — $3.25
- ☐ MC44768-8 My Secret Admirer — $3.25
- ☐ MC47101-5 Silent Witness — $3.25
- ☐ MC46044-7 The Stepdaughter — $3.25
- ☐ MC44916-8 The Window — $3.25

Lael Littke
- ☐ MC44237-6 Prom Dress — $3.50

Jane McFann
- ☐ MC46690-9 Be Mine — $3.25

Christopher Pike
- ☐ MC43014-9 Slumber Party — $3.50
- ☐ MC44256-2 Weekend — $3.50

Edited by T. Pines
- ☐ MC45256-8 Thirteen — $3.99

Sinclair Smith
- ☐ MC45063-8 The Waitress — $3.50

Barbara Steiner
- ☐ MC46425-6 The Phantom — $3.50

Robert Westall
- ☐ MC41693-6 Ghost Abbey — $3.25
- ☐ MC43761-5 The Promise — $3.25
- ☐ MC45176-6 Yaxley's Cat — $3.25

Available wherever you buy books, or use this order form.

Scholastic Inc., P.O. Box 7502, 2931 East McCarty Street, Jefferson City, MO 65102

Please send me the books I have checked above. I am enclosing $_____ (please add $2.00 to cover shipping and handling). Send check or money order — no cash or C.O.D.s please.

Name _____ Age _____

Address_____

City_____ State/Zip_____

Please allow four to six weeks for delivery. Offer good in the U.S. only. Sorry, mail orders are not available to residents of Canada. Prices subject to change.

T295